"Put your leg...

Her eyebrows ... ...et me go! You are...

"Your choice, ...risa," he said, stepping away. "Good luck."

"No, wait," she cried out as he started down the sidewalk. When he stopped, she let out a harsh breath. "Okay, I'll do it your way."

She wrapped her arms around his neck, obeying without argument this time. Alexei cupped her thighs, pushed into the cradle of her hips. His coat was long and hid their bodies from view. If they did this right, anyone seeing them would think they were having sex.

She was small, soft, and she smelled like summer in the Urals—a hint of flowers, sunshine, and cool water. Anger flashed through him. Her scent made him remember, made him feel. He didn't like feeling. He had no room for feeling.

Feeling made you weak, had the power to break you.

"Kiss me," he growled as the footsteps pounded closer. "And make it believable."

Lynn Raye Harris read her first Mills & Boon® Romance when her grandmother carted home a box from a yard sale. She didn't know she wanted to be a writer then, but she definitely knew she wanted to marry a sheikh or a prince and live the glamorous life she read about in the pages. Instead she married a military man, and moved around the world. These days she makes her home in North Alabama, with her handsome husband and two crazy cats. Writing for Harlequin is a dream come true. You can visit her at www.lynnrayeharris.com

PRINCE VORONOV'S VIRGIN

BY
LYNN RAYE HARRIS

MILLS & BOON

First published in Great Britain 2011
Harlequin Mills & Boon Limited,
Eton House, 18-24 Paradise Road, Richmond, Surrey TW9 1SR

© Lynn Raye Harris 2011

ISBN: 978 0 263 88626 9

Harlequin Mills & Boon policy is to use papers that are natural, renewable and recyclable products and made from wood grown in sustainable forests. The logging and manufacturing process conform to the legal environmental regulations of the country of origin.

Printed and bound in Spain
by Litografia Rosés, S.A., Barcelona

PRINCE VORONOV'S VIRGIN

To Mom, who took me to St. Petersburg and Moscow many years ago, and who has always been fascinated with all things Russian.

CHAPTER ONE

THE SCREAM THAT SPLIT the night arrowed down Alexei Voronov's spine like a river of ice water. His senses throttled into high alert. A light snow fell steadily, dusting the cobblestones of Red Square. To the right, the Kremlin wall bordered the square. At the far end, the Spassky Tower, with its giant clock like Big Ben in London, stood out like a beacon, as did the colorful onion domes of St. Basil's nearby.

But the hour was late, and there was no movement in the square.

Until the scream echoed again.

Alexei swore. He'd been standing in the shadows of the Russian museum, waiting for his contact to arrive, but he couldn't ignore the cry. Though it was probably a fight in one of the nearby clubs, a woman screaming bloody murder while her man fought for her honor, he had to act. It was going to cost him valuable information since his contact wouldn't wait around once he discovered Alexei wasn't there.

Then again, he'd been waiting for the last half hour and the man was already fifteen minutes late. In truth, Alexei had begun to wonder if the other man had changed his mind.

It was possible.

If Alexei's adversary had got wind of his intentions, he might have paid the informant more. Though Alexei had been about to pay him a fortune. Still, he couldn't stand around and wait while a woman needed help.

Just his damned luck to be cursed with a nobility gene, even at the expense of his own best interests. He was ruthless in everything he did—except when someone was in physical danger.

Across the square from the Kremlin, the GUM department store shone brightly. Alexei started in that direction but stopped when he heard a noise. Footsteps? The echo in the empty square made it difficult to pinpoint their direction.

Before he could figure it out, a woman bolted out of the darkness. He had no time to step out of her path. She plowed into him, nearly knocking them both to the pavement.

Alexei caught her close, steadied her as he took a step backward to brace himself. It was like trying to hold a jaguar. She made no noise, but she shoved against him with all her strength, her elbow darting up toward his face. Instinctively he deflected the blow, then spun her until her back was to him, clamping a hand tightly over her mouth.

He could feel the scream gathering in her throat as he dragged her hard against him. If he let go, she'd shatter his eardrums.

"If you scream again," he said very coolly in her ear, "whoever is chasing you will find you. And I won't get in the middle of your lovers' quarrel."

Why couldn't he, for once, stay out of it? It was later than the appointed time, but his informant could still arrive. A major business deal was at stake, not to mention years of working toward a single goal that was nearly within his grasp. Missing a meeting for the sake of what was most likely a drunken spat was not part of the plan. He could turn around now and be back to the museum in a few strides.

The woman's voice was muffled as she tried to shake her head. It occurred to him she might be a tourist. There were many tourists in Moscow these days, unlike in the old days when he was growing up. He repeated it in English, just in case.

He felt the sharp intake of her breath, knew he'd guessed right. He also spoke German, French and Polish, but English had seemed the most expedient choice since nearly everyone spoke it as a second language.

"I won't hurt you," he said. "But if you scream, I will let him have you. Understand?"

She gave a quick nod as he turned her in his arms again. Her smoky eyes shimmered in the reflected light of the store. Her jacket hood had fallen back, revealing dark hair caught in a thick ponytail. Her features were fine, delicate, though the elbow she'd aimed at his head had been anything but weak. She was strong, this woman. Strong and delicate at once.

Alexei pulled his hand away from her mouth. Her expression was wary but she didn't scream.

"Please help me," she blurted, wrapping her arms around herself to ward off the late April chill. "Don't let them take me."

American.

He shouldn't be surprised, and yet something about her was wholly unexpected. Such as what an American woman who spoke no Russian was doing alone in Red Square at nearly one in the morning.

Don't get involved, Alexei.

He shoved the voice aside and concentrated on her. "Don't let who take you? The authorities? If you've done something illegal, I can't help you."

"No," she said, casting her gaze behind her before turning to him again. "It's nothing like that. I'm looking for my sister and—"

Angry shouts rang through the square. She didn't wait for his answer; she simply bolted into the night as if shot from a cannon. Alexei caught her in three strides, clamping a hand over her arm and spinning her around.

"This way," he said, hauling her toward the department store.

"It's too bright. They'll see us."

"Precisely."

Boots clomped over the cobbles, coming toward them. They had only seconds before the men made it down the hill. The slick snow was hindering them, but not much. Alexei shoved the girl back against one of the huge plate windows. She made a sound of protest.

"Put your legs around me."

Her eyebrows shot toward her hairline. "Let me go! You aren't trying to help at all—"

"Your choice, *maya krasavitsa*," he said, stepping away. "Good luck."

"No, wait," she cried out as he started down the sidewalk. When he stopped, she let out a harsh breath. "Okay, I'll do it your way."

Alexei gave her a smile he knew was anything but friendly. "*Speciba*. We will pretend to be lovers, yes? Put your legs around me," he said as he crowded her against the window and pulled her hair free of its confinement. She wrapped her arms around his neck, obeying without argument this time. Alexei cupped her thighs, pushed into the cradle of her hips. His coat was long and hid their bodies from view. If they did this right, anyone seeing them would think they were having sex.

The American bit back a soft moan as he pushed harder against her most sensitive spot. The sound crashed through his veins like a shot of vodka. No matter how he willed it otherwise, his body was reacting.

Chert poberi.

She was small, soft and she smelled like summer in the

Urals—a hint of flowers, sunshine and cool water. Anger flashed through him. Her scent made him remember, made him feel. He didn't like feeling. He had no room for feeling.

Feeling made you weak, had the power to break you.

"Kiss me," he growled as the footsteps pounded closer. "And make it believable."

Paige blinked up at the dark stranger holding her so intimately. My God, how had she found herself in this mess? She should have gone straight to Chad the instant Emma came up missing. But she'd thought her sister had simply forgotten the time. And Paige wasn't about to disrupt her boss's evening when he'd been kind enough to allow her to bring Emma along on this trip in the first place.

Chad Russell was one of Dallas's most eligible bachelors. He was cool, handsome and wealthy. And she was his secretary. Or at least she was for this trip, since his executive secretary wasn't allowed to fly longer than three hours at a time per her doctor's orders. Mavis had a clotting disorder that could be fatal if she spent a lot of time on planes, so Paige had gotten this assignment when Chad had to choose a secretary for the trip.

She'd been thrilled, and determined to do the best job possible since he'd chosen her over some of the other secretaries with more experience. No, Chad had enough to worry about without also taking on the problem of his junior secretary's younger sister. He was here to close a major deal, not to track down an irresponsible twenty-one-year-old.

And Paige was here to prove she could handle more responsibility and that she was an asset to Russell Tech.

Lately she'd even thought Chad might be interested in her as more than just an employee. She'd tried not to read anything into his actions, but he'd taken her to lunch twice—and he'd asked about her personal life, about her sister, about many things other than work. Her heart had pounded the whole time. Chad was everything she'd ever thought attractive in a man. She'd had a small crush on him since the first moment he'd walked into the office and smiled at her nearly two years ago.

Until now she'd never thought it was anything more than futile.

Tonight, she'd let her feelings get in the way of her common sense. She should have followed her instincts and asked for Chad's help. But she was so accustomed to solving her own problems that she'd dismissed her uneasiness and was determined to find Emma on her own. And now she was kicking herself for it.

"There is no time to waste," the stranger growled.

His voice was deep, rich, the rolling of the vowels across his tongue a thing of beauty. His accent wasn't heavy, but it was distinctly Russian.

Paige's heart flipped in her chest as he squeezed her tighter. She had to find Emma. But first she had to survive the next few minutes. And to do that, she feared she had to do as he asked. What other choice was there? The men she'd run from outnumbered them. If they caught her, she might not escape a second time.

Not that she really knew what they wanted. She'd wandered too far from the hotel, gotten lost and stumbled into a group of men who'd frightened her. They'd been drinking, and they'd not been too willing to help. Or not without a price. She shuddered as she thought of the blond giant with the meaty hands who'd told her in thick Russian that he'd help her if she would kiss him.

Then he'd laughed, and the others had joined in. The sound was ugly and made the hair on her arms prickle. But it wasn't until he'd grabbed her that she'd screamed. She'd bought herself a little time with the well-aimed kick to his groin. While the others scrambled to help him, she'd run.

Why she now believed *this* man was truly trying to help her, she wasn't sure. But she was positive he was—or at least he was the lesser of two evils, if the way her senses were reeling was any indication. The simple contact of body on body, of his groin pressed intimately to hers in spite of the layers of clothing between them, had her heart thundering, her nerve endings tingling.

She wanted to know who he was, why he was helping her, but there was no time to ask. The stranger's ice-gray eyes gazed down at her, urging her to comply. The heavy clomp of boots on the cobbles grew louder.

In an instant, Paige closed her eyes and fused her lips to his. She decided at the last second that she would keep her mouth closed. There was no reason to truly kiss him, was there? The appearance of it would surely be enough to fool these men.

But the stranger wouldn't allow it. His tongue slid along the seam of her lips. She gasped at the heat and surprise of the movement.

That little gasp was all he needed to slip his tongue into her mouth. Her heart hammered as he kissed her with such expertise that her knees would have buckled had she been standing.

He tasted like brandy and mint, so masculine and strong, and she was shocked at the languidness stealing across her senses. He wasn't Chad, wasn't the man she'd fantasized about for the past two years—but she wanted to lose herself in his embrace, wanted to see what kind of magic he could make if they were alone together and naked.

Except she hadn't the first clue *how* to make magic with a man, truth be told. In the last eight years, she'd had exactly one sexual experience—and that hadn't been anything to write home about. Becoming a single parent to a sister when you were only eighteen, and then working your way through school and trying to support a household, didn't leave much time for dating or building relationships.

But not one of the handful of kisses she'd ever experienced had been anything like this. *This* kiss was incredible. And it did things to her insides. She felt liquid and hot. Like the fireworks bursting in her body had turned into a single living flame.

Paige felt heat and passion so strongly that it shocked her. How could she be so responsive at a time like this?

The man growled low in his throat, squeezed her tighter to him as the kiss slid over the edge.

Paige wasn't herself. It was the only explanation. She was no longer a dull secretary working for a man she could never have, no longer the responsible older sister who took care of everything. She was hot, sensual, and completely in charge of her destiny. She was living a life of international intrigue and danger, an exciting life filled with passion and amazing men who spoke Russian-accented English and kissed the living daylights out of her.

Voices sounded close by, bringing her back to reality. And then a wolf-whistle. Paige's heart dived into her stomach.

"Don't be frightened," the stranger whispered against the column of her throat as he maneuvered her face away from the side the men were on. "They will go soon."

She trembled in answer, though it wasn't from fear as his mouth glided near her ear again.

"What is your name?"

It startled her, that question. He was pressed against her so intimately, his lips moving across her skin as if they'd been born to do so, the ridge of an impressive erection riding the crease in her thighs, and he didn't even know her name. If the situation weren't so insane, she'd have laughed.

He flexed his hips and sensation bolted through her. If he kept doing that, oh...

"Your name," he said against her cheekbone.

"Paige," she said in the instant before his mouth claimed hers again.

The whistles grew louder, and then a voice said something sharp and they stopped. The voice said something again, louder and sharper. She felt the stranger's muscles tighten.

The other man spoke in Russian, a question by the way he left the statement hanging at the end. The truth hit her like a blast of icy water. He was questioning *them*. Paige's breath drew in sharply.

"Moan," the stranger said against her lips.

The word was so foreign to her, so heavy with meaning. His accent scraped over the word, made it seem both harder and sexier than anything she'd ever heard in her life.

He squeezed her thighs hard, and she realized they were in danger, that he knew it, too. Somehow, the fact he was aware of the danger made it seem bigger, more real. They were completely outnumbered. If these men realized who she was, if they decided to finish what they'd started, the stranger would be no help against so many.

Paige pulled her mouth from his, buried her face against his neck and let out the best moan she could. The sound was weak, unconvincing.

"Louder," he said in her ear, his hips flexing once more against her center.

Sensation caught, held, spun her in its grip as he ground against her. The moan that left her lips this time was very real. His mouth sought hers again. His kiss was warm, hard and demanding. Paige threaded her fingers in the hair at his nape, toyed with the soft edge of the fur cap he wore.

With the pressure of his body centered on her most sensitive spot, he drove her toward something she'd never actually experienced with a man. They were clothed, and yet she was about to splinter apart.

She'd been so deprived and now—oh now the floodgates had been opened. They weren't even naked, weren't really intimate in any way, and she felt so much.

She moaned again, gasping as his hand cupped her breast through her shirt. His thumb slid over her nipple; he made a noise when he realized it was a hard little point. The sound of his voice rocked her, kicked up her senses.

Unbelievably she was almost there, almost to that peak of sensation. She felt wicked, hot and utterly desperate.

It was wrong, wrong, and yet—

The stranger tore his mouth from hers and put distance between them. He still supported her, but they were no longer so tightly pressed together. He looked completely unaffected by what had just happened while she was hot and cold and frustrated all at once.

And then she remembered. Her gaze shot over his shoulder as confusion gave way to panic. He'd decided to give her up, decided she wasn't worth helping—

"They are gone," he said. He eased her legs down his hips until she was standing. Released from his grip, she felt so cold all of a sudden. She wrapped her arms around her body. Her teeth started to chatter softly, but she couldn't seem to stop.

"Thank you," she said, strangely disappointed that she hadn't tumbled over that peak after all. Her body still hummed with the aftereffects of too much adrenaline, too much thwarted pleasure.

"*Ne ze chto.* Now we must go."

Paige blinked up at him, looking at him fully for the first time—and nearly sank to the cold ground in shock. He was a stunning man. Hollywood handsome in a way that screamed bad boy, playboy. Except he wasn't a boy at all. It struck her how incongruous those terms were to describe a man like him.

She'd been so focused before, so scared, that she'd barely registered any details about him.

Now, she took them in. Every last incredible line. Beneath his cap, he had dark thick hair that was probably brown but looked black in the lights, and the kind of nose and cheekbones that artists had been sculpting out of marble for hundreds of years. His lips were full, sensual, his jaw strong. He watched her with glacial eyes that missed nothing.

And he'd just told her they needed to leave. Together.

Paige backed up a step, suddenly confused and wary. She'd made too many mistakes already. She'd come this far from her hotel without a plan, and nearly been assaulted. Going anywhere with this man was out of the question, no matter how much she might owe him for helping her.

"I appreciate your help, and I'd be happy to pay you, but if you think I'm going somewhere with you to finish—"

His expression grew absolutely stony. "You think too highly of yourself, Paige. And you will come with me now if you wish to avoid a repeat scenario. Those men could return to the square in five minutes, when they've realized you didn't go into the subway or any of the open clubs."

"I'll return to my hotel. It's just down the street—"

"It's not safe."

"My boss is there and he can help—"

"No," he cut in. "It will be safer if you come with me now."

The slow burn of anger began in her belly. Who was he to tell her what to do? And what did he mean it wasn't safe? It had to be safer than going with him! "I appreciate your help, but my sister is *missing* and I think Chad is the only one who can help me—"

He took a step closer, every inch of him suddenly on alert. "Chad? Chad Russell is your boss?"

Paige bit her lip, uncertain whether this was a good or a bad sign. "You know Chad?"

His laugh was not precisely friendly. "Indeed, I know Chad Russell, *maya krasavitsa*. And I know that you had better come with me now, if you want to survive this night."

Paige shivered. Something in his tone made her want to back away. "I'm not sure that's a good idea," she said.

He glared at her until she was certain he would grab her bodily and force her to go whether she wanted to or not. But then he shrugged. "It is your life. Do what you wish."

"But why? Why isn't it safe?" she demanded, her heart racing.

His mouth twisted disdainfully. "The streets are not safe at night, as you have so recently discovered. This is true of many big cities, I understand."

She felt like he was mocking her, and yet there was some sense to what he said. Would she walk the streets of downtown Dallas alone at night? Definitely not.

"I can pay you to take me back to the hotel."

His bark of laughter was not what she expected. Her face burned, as if she'd insulted him somehow and embarrassed herself in the process. God, what a strange night!

"Come with me, or go your own way. The choice is yours." He didn't wait for her to reply. He simply turned and started down the hill in the direction the men had gone. Paige chewed her lip, shivering and wondering what in the hell she should do now.

Maybe she could make it back alone, assuming she didn't get lost again. Her hotel was through the square and down the road that ran along the Moscow River. It was a long walk. Cold. Dark.

She would run. She could make it in ten minutes if she hurried. Maybe Emma had already returned. If not, Chad was there to help.

The sound of male voices, speaking in Russian, filtered to her on the night air. Their speech was loud and punctuated with laughter. She didn't know if it was the same men who'd tried to grab her, but could she risk it?

Paige pressed the heels of her hands to her temples. Oh, God, what was she doing here? Why had she thought she could handle this alone? She didn't speak the language, and sometimes didn't even understand the thickly accented English that was spoken to her. Her eyes strained to see the figure of the man disappearing into the night. She understood him.

But he was a stranger. How could she go anywhere with a man she didn't know?

The Russian voices grew louder as they moved closer to where she still stood in front of the department store. Given a choice between meeting up with these men, or going with the man who'd helped her, she realized the truth: there was no choice.

Paige broke into a run.

CHAPTER TWO

ALEXEI POURED SCOTCH into a tumbler and handed it to the woman sitting so forlornly on his couch. The walk through the cold city streets had chilled her, he was certain, but a stiff drink would bring her around. And then he would find out why she'd been in Red Square at the precise time he'd been supposed to meet with his informant. Considering she was one of Chad Russell's employees, it was quite a coincidence.

He did not believe in coincidences. Hard work and sacrifice had gotten him where he was today, not belief in mystical concurrences. If he'd left his life up to luck and circumstance, he'd probably be lying in a crypt with the rest of his family.

She accepted the glass without looking and took a big drink. Then she coughed. "That's horrible!"

Alexei sipped his own scotch, enjoying the notes of caramel and oak as it slid down his throat. The fifty-year-old single malt was perfect. And so was her performance. She definitely knew how to play the innocent.

His mouth twisted in disdain.

Like his father before him, Chad Russell had always believed he could ruin Voronov Exploration if he threw enough money at the right people. He hadn't yet succeeded, nor would he.

Alexei would die before he would lose the next round in their epic battle. Whoever could convince Pyotr Valishnikov to sell his Baltic and Siberian holdings first would reap a huge reward—and effectively leave the other company in the metaphorical dust. This deal was the culmination of everything Alexei had ever worked for. With the stroke of a pen, Valishnikov could give him the power to finally crush Russell Tech once and for all.

Then Katerina would be avenged. It was all that mattered.

Alexei studied the woman on his couch.

Was she here to dig up information about his plans? If so, she would be sorely disappointed. But if she was supposed to distract him enough to let down his guard, she wasn't doing the best job of it. She was beautiful, though in an unstudied way. He'd known many beautiful women over the years, but this one seemed quite unaware of her beauty. She hadn't once tried to fix her hair or asked to see a mirror so she could primp and preen. Her makeup was so understated as to be practically nonexistent.

And she seemed to be in shock, which was why he'd given her the scotch.

As he watched, she reached into one of the pockets of her very unstylish coat and pulled out a pair of glasses. Then she glanced up at him and shrugged as she put them on.

"I can see pretty well without them, but I get headaches if I go too long." She dropped her gaze to the glass in her hand. "They fogged up when I went outside and I just never put them back on."

"What were you doing in Red Square alone?"

She looked up at him again, her dark eyes shiny with unshed tears. Once more, he got that little kick in the gut he'd felt earlier when he'd breathed in her scent. His sister'd had dark eyes like those. Dark, haunting eyes that he couldn't escape, no matter how successful he became or how much he tried to put the past behind him.

"I don't even know your name," she said numbly.

"Alexei," he replied. He did not doubt that she knew exactly who he was. Perhaps he should have taken her up on her offer to return her to her hotel. He hadn't believed it was genuine at the time, nor did he now. But what would she have done if he'd said yes? That would have caused a bit of consternation, he was certain. When he'd first told her she needed to come with him, before he'd known who she was, he'd had every intention of driving her back to her hotel once he'd reached his apartment.

Afterward, it had seemed unnecessary—not to mention counterintuitive to her plan. He wondered why she'd even told him she worked for Chad Russell in the first place.

"Alexei," she repeated.

"*Da.* Now tell me about your sister."

He would play her game. For now.

Panic threaded into those smoky eyes. She took another swig of scotch, coughed. If she was acting, she was doing a fine job of it.

"Emma's twenty-one, as of yesterday. She's nothing like me. She's tall and blonde, and she likes to have fun and go shopping. She went on a guided tour this afternoon while I worked to prepare Chad's papers for his meeting tomorrow. I ate dinner in Chad's suite while we worked, and stayed with him until about eight-thirty. I had a text from Emma around eight, telling me she would be in the hotel bar for a while. She wasn't in our room when I got back, but I didn't think anything of it until she didn't return by eleven. I tried calling her, but she never answered."

The twinge of feeling he got when he thought of this woman with Russell surprised him. Because he doubted very much that she'd simply been *working* with her boss all that time. A beautiful woman like her with a man like Russell?

He'd lay odds they'd been doing far more than going over paperwork.

She plunked the tumbler on the table and stood. But she must have gotten up too quickly because the color drained from her face and she sank back down again. Then she put a hand to her head.

"I don't usually drink alcohol," she said more to herself than to him. She looked up again, her eyes slightly glazed. How could anyone get drunk on two gulps of scotch? "I have to find her," she whispered.

"I will find her for you," Alexei said smoothly. Let her believe her plan was working. "You looked for her in this bar?"

She clasped both hands in her lap, her knuckles whitening. "Yes. I asked if anyone had seen her, but they claimed not to remember."

"So you decided to wander alone through Red Square at midnight?"

Her eyes were huge and liquid. "It was stupid, I know. But I thought she couldn't have gone far, thought maybe she was outside. And then someone said there was another bar, so I went there. Each place I went was farther than the last until I found myself in the square and those men started bothering me."

"Where is your cell phone?"

She patted her coat, came up empty. "I think I dropped it when they grabbed me."

Alexei took his phone from his jacket and handed it to her. "Try to call your sister."

She punched in a few numbers. He could hear the error message on the other end as she handed the phone back, her expression a mixture of frustration and fear. "I don't know how to dial it from a foreign number."

"Tell me the number." He punched it in while she recited

it, adding the proper codes, then handed the phone back when it began to ring. Her face screwed up while she concentrated, as if she were willing her sister—assuming there really was a sister—to answer.

It didn't work, however, because she gave the phone back to him a moment later, her expression crumpling.

Alexei dialed another number. After issuing instructions to his head of personal security, he hung up.

"Why don't you give me your coat? I will turn on the fire to warm you."

"I really should be going," she said, her pretty bow mouth drawing his attention as her teeth scraped her bottom lip worriedly.

Alexei tried very hard to ignore the arrow of arousal that shot straight to his groin. She'd been uncertain earlier, but she'd warmed up to their kiss, coming alive beneath his touch. It had been everything he could do to push her away when all he'd wanted was to sample the rest of her. To see if the fire in that kiss would translate to the bedroom.

Odd, when she wasn't his usual type of woman. He liked glamorous women, effortlessly feminine women who wore their confidence like a second skin. Paige was neither glamorous nor confident, though she was definitely feminine. *Authentic* was the word that came to mind—though of course that couldn't be the case when she was working for Chad Russell. She was simply a very good actress.

"It is safer to remain here," he said. "In case those men are looking for you."

She blinked. "How could that be? They don't know me—"

"Your phone."

Her eyes widened. "I hadn't thought of that. I still don't know why they'd care." She shook her head suddenly. "But they wouldn't. And I need to find my sister, so I should go back—"

"I will find your sister, I promise." He said it impatiently, since she couldn't really want to leave yet, but she didn't seem to notice.

She blinked at him, her eyes adorably owlish behind her glasses. "Do you really think you can find her?"

He nodded. "You arc in Russia, *mayu krasavitsa,* and I am Russian. I guarantee I will find her before your Chad could do so."

Real hope kindled in the depths of those eyes. It made him wonder, for an instant, if he was wrong about her motives for being here.

That is exactly what you are supposed to think.

He shoved the thought aside, but not before he pictured another set of eyes gazing at him with hope. *Katerina, I'm sorry...*

A cold hand gripped his, pulling him back to the present. He didn't mind the cold. It was the touch of her skin that surprised him. The jolt must have surprised her as well, because she quickly pulled away.

"Thank you, Alexei," she said in that soft, breathy voice that reminded him of film stars of the 1940s. "You have been very kind. I don't know what would have happened if you hadn't been there."

If the whole scenario hadn't been a setup, then he knew exactly what could have happened—and it wasn't pretty.

"You must never go out alone at night in a strange city where you do not speak the language or understand the culture." He said it rather harshly, he thought, but she merely nodded.

"You're right, of course." She sank back against the cushions and closed her eyes. When she didn't open them again, he grew concerned. A moment later, her jaw dropped open and a soft snore escaped.

Alexei stood there for a moment in disbelief. Tossing back the rest of his scotch, he decided to turn the lights down and leave her where she was. If she were here to spy, she'd be up in no time. All he had to do was wait and see.

Paige was warm and cozy. Something soft nestled against her cheek as she stirred. She smiled, sighing as she burrowed deeper beneath the cover. The hotel bed was comfortable, but it felt different tonight than it had the night before. Firmer. And why was she still wearing her clothes?

A tendril of unease twisted through her. Something wasn't right. Her eyes popped open—a second later, she bolted upright. Her gaze darted around the room, but nothing was familiar.

Where was she?

Her surroundings were luxurious—the couch she lay on was covered in silk brocade, oil paintings adorned the walls and the cover she'd been snuggling into was made out of some kind of fur.

A fire burned softly in the grate, the only sound in the room. Paige stood, wrapping the blanket around her though she was still fully clothed, and turned in a circle. She didn't have a watch, and she'd lost her cell phone in the square. She had no idea what time it was, or whether Emma had been found.

How had she managed to fall asleep when she was so worried?

"Alexei?"

She started walking toward a hallway directly behind her. It might be late, but she couldn't simply sit on the couch and wait until morning. She had to know if Alexei had found Emma.

The thought of her enigmatic rescuer sent a wave of a

different kind of heat rolling over her. She'd been wary when he'd first told her she needed to go with him, but once they arrived at his apartment, she'd realized he had money. This apartment was in one of the old Baroque buildings that had withstood time, several wars and a revolution. It was also furnished with expensive paintings, antiques and woven rugs.

And he knew Chad, though she still didn't know how he did, come to think of it.

But she'd relaxed a little then. Surely he did not need to lure poor American women back to his apartment for evil purposes. No doubt women fell all over a man who looked like he did. Add in the money, and you had a sure recipe for success.

No, Alexei did not need to bring her here in order to have his wicked way with her. He'd kissed her because it was necessary, not because he was attracted to her.

Paige lifted her chin. Nor was she attracted to him. He was a handsome man, no doubt, but he wasn't Chad. Chad was tall, blond, Texan, bigger than life. Everything she'd ever dreamed about when she was a girl growing up in tiny Atkinsville, Texas.

She knew that Chad taking her to lunch—and picking her to accompany him on this trip—might not mean anything, but a girl could dream. Though he usually dated underwear models, actresses and beauty queens, he wasn't seeing anyone just now. She knew because she was the one who usually got the task of ordering the flowers and making the dinner reservations. There had been none of those for over a month now.

Not that it meant anything, she reminded herself, when he'd been working nonstop on this Russian deal.

A lamp burned in one of the rooms off the hallway. Paige pushed the door all the way open. "Alexei?"

There was no answer, but she stepped inside to be sure he wasn't there anyway. The room was an office, with floor to ceiling bookcases, a desk and filing cabinets. A computer stood on the desk, and a printer sat idle nearby. There was an Italian leather couch on one wall, and a couple of chairs facing it.

But no one was inside. She turned to leave, biting off a scream as a man stepped through the door.

"Looking for something?"

Paige put a hand to her racing heart. "You scared me."

"Apparently," he said, though there was no amusement in his voice.

"I was looking for you."

One dark eyebrow arched. "Really? Why?"

Paige swallowed. He stood before her in jeans and an unbuttoned white shirt, as if he'd hurriedly pulled it on. His feet were bare, and his hair was mussed. She resolutely focused on his face instead of the naked skin of his chest and abdomen. Or the shadowed indentations of muscle and sinew.

"I'm sorry if I woke you. But I have no idea what time it is. If Emma returned to our room by now, she'll be worried. I really should go…" Her voice tapered off as she realized she was babbling.

"Your sister is not in your room."

Paige felt her heart skip a painful beat. She took a step toward him, thought better of it and clutched the blanket tighter instead. "How do you know? Do you know where she is?"

"*Da.* She is safe, Paige. You have nothing to worry about."

Relief threatened to buckle her knees.

Alexei reached for her as she swayed, caught her in a strong grip. Then he ushered her to the couch and sat her down. "You are quite good at this," he murmured.

Paige blinked up at him. "I'm sorry?"

He turned away and went over to a cabinet close by, returned with a glass and thrust it toward her.

Paige held up her hand as her stomach rebelled. "Not again—"

"It is water."

She took the glass and drank, thankful because her mouth was suddenly so dry. Her head felt light, and her heart thundered in her chest. She'd promised Mama that she'd take good care of Emma. Her sister had only been thirteen when their mother died, and Paige had done her best. If Emma was a bit spoiled, a bit irresponsible, it was Paige's fault for indulging her.

She'd been trying to make up for the lack of parents, but she hadn't done the best job. Tonight, she thought she'd failed utterly. To know that Emma was safe filled her with a profound sense of relief.

"Where is she?"

"She is with Chad Russell, as you very well know."

"Oh thank God," Paige breathed. Though what made him think she knew where Emma was?

Before she could ask, Alexei's cool silver gaze pierced her. "Why are you here?"

Paige blinked. "I was looking for you—"

"No, I mean why are you here, in my home?"

It took her a moment to formulate an answer. "Because you told me I had to come with you."

"Yes, but *why* did you do so? What did you hope to find? Is Russell so desperate he would send a secretary to spy on me?"

Confusion crashed through her. And a thread of simmering anger.

"Why would I want to spy on you? I don't even know you!" She set the glass aside and stood, tilting her chin up. It

was simply a show of bravado since she was shaking inside
her skin. But she'd learned at an early age to bluff her way
through the rough spots when necessary. Or, as her mother
used to say, *never let them see you sweat.* She'd had plenty of
practice when Child Services had come calling to see if she
was capable of taking care of her sister or if Emma needed
to go into foster care instead.

"Stop pretending you don't know who I am," he com-
manded.

Paige stomped her foot. It was childish, she knew, but it
was instinctive. She couldn't stop herself whenever she was
angry or nervous—though anger was not the dominant emotion at the moment.

"You are Alexei, a man I met in Red Square, who helped
me when I was in trouble. You obviously have money, and
you knew who Chad was as soon as I mentioned him. But I
have no idea who you are."

It was a troubling thought, not to know the man who
seemed to know so much about you.

He closed the distance between them, slipped an arm
around her waist beneath the blanket. His fingers traced her
jaw, slid into the hair at her nape. "You are a fascinating
woman, Paige. No wonder Russell chose you for this task.
Or did you volunteer?"

With a tug, she was flush against him. The blanket fell
away as she let it go to press her hands against his chest. Paige
closed her eyes. His *naked* chest.

His skin was hot beneath her hands, silky and hard, and
she longed to stroke it.

Stop it. How could she possibly find him sexy at a time
like this?

"Let me go," she breathed.

"Before you've done what you came to do?"

"I didn't come here to do *anything*."

"What did Russell offer you?"

"I don't know what you're talking about!"

"Were you supposed to seduce me? Supposed to leave me sated and exhausted in bed while you went through my papers?" His head dipped toward her. "Because I have to say, Paige, that I am very disappointed in your technique thus far. But I find I am quite willing to allow you to complete your mission."

She knew she should pull away when his lips touched hers, but it was physically impossible. Not because he held her too tightly, but because her body was zinging with sparks that she didn't want to end.

His tongue slipped into her mouth, and she met him stroke for stroke. He smelled so good, like spice and a cold winter night, yet he was as hot as a volcanic eruption. His skin sizzled into her where she touched him with her bare hands. She wanted to slip the shirt from his shoulders, wanted to see if his skin tasted as good as it felt.

His hands slid into her hair, tugged her head back. His mouth left hers, forged a trail of fire along her jaw, the column of her throat.

Her head fell to one side, giving him greater access. He made a sound of approval, and she opened her eyes—just for a moment—and found herself staring at the most erotic scene she'd ever personally experienced. A mirror on the opposite wall caught their reflection, shone it back at her.

It was like a scene out of a movie. A gorgeous man held a woman in his embrace, a woman whose dark hair flowed wildly over her shoulders, whose eyes sparkled with passion as the man's mouth moved across her skin.

It was exotic and beautiful.

And she wasn't supposed to be the woman in the scene. This man didn't care for her. He thought Chad had sent her here to seduce him, for God's sake—which was a laugh in itself—and she had no idea *who* he really was.

Paige's hands curled into fists against his hard chest.

And then she pushed. "Stop. Please stop."

Amazingly he did. Alexei's eyes were hot, glittering as he straightened to his full height and glared down at her. He was even taller than Chad, broader, and he did things to her insides—

Stop thinking about it.

Paige closed her eyes, took a step back. Her clothes were intact, but she felt as if he'd undressed her, as if he knew all her secrets.

A ridiculous feeling, really. He might know her name, and he might know she was Chad's secretary, but he did not know *her.*

"I want to go back to my hotel," she said with as much dignity as she could summon. "Chad has a very important meeting tomorrow, and I have to be there. He needs me. And Emma will be wondering where I am by now."

Alexei shoved a hand through his thick hair—black, not brown, she realized. "You will not be going anywhere tonight."

"I want to see my sister," she insisted. "You have no right to keep me here."

His gaze sharpened. "Your sister is busy, Paige. I doubt she will want to be disturbed. Though perhaps you did not know you were sharing your lover with her?"

Everything inside her went cold and still. "My lover?" she said numbly.

"You never give up the pretense, do you?"

She ignored him, her mind beginning to work overtime. Emma and Chad? They'd met once or twice when Emma had come to the office, but Chad hadn't shown any particular interest in her sister.

Or had he?

She remembered Emma's flirtatious giggle, Chad's mega-watt smile, Emma's declaration later that night that Chad was probably amazing in bed. She'd thought the same thing herself, but she figured she'd never know.

She just hadn't realized that Emma might actually find out.

Chad had suggested she bring Emma along on this trip when Paige expressed disappointment she would be gone for her sister's twenty-first birthday. She'd thought he was being kind. She'd refused at first until he insisted it would be fine, that he wouldn't hear of them being separated for Emma's birthday.

And now this.

Paige put a hand on the bookcase to steady herself. Rage, disappointment, betrayal—they whirled inside her like a hurricane, spinning her in a vortex of emotion. She'd thought he was interested in her, when all along it had been Emma! She'd been so stupid, so blind.

Chad and Emma. Her boss and her sister. Making love while she searched the icy Moscow streets in a panic. Making love while she nearly got assaulted by a group of drunken men.

Her sister making love with the man *she* wanted, the man she'd secretly been in love with forever.

Tears pressed against the backs of her eyes. She would not let them fall, not now. Not here, not in front of Alexei.

"Paige," he said, taking her arm.

She jerked away and hugged her arms tightly around her body. "Leave me alone."

"I apologize if this news hurts you."

She speared him with a glare. A blurry glare, since her eyes were swimming in moisture. "You don't care, so spare me your insincerity. Besides, how do I know you're telling the truth? How could you possibly have found Emma if she's in Chad's room?"

What if he'd made the whole thing up? Though why he would do so, she couldn't say, but surely it was a possibility.

"My head of security used to work for the secret police," he replied softly. "Yuri knows people, and he knows how to get things done. But I can certainly prove where your sister is if you wish. My men have audio of her with—"

"Stop," she blurted, turning away, her body trembling with anger and pain. Her intuition had told her all along he was telling the truth, which was why she'd reacted, but that hadn't stopped her from grasping at straws. The last thing she wanted to hear was Chad and Emma whispering together in bed. Or worse.

Before she realized what Alexei was about to do, he wrapped her in his embrace, his hand pressing against the back of her head so that her cheek was flush against his bare chest. Briefly she considered struggling—but gave up the idea as his other hand rhythmically rubbed her back.

It'd been a long time since anyone had comforted her. She was always the one doing the comforting, the one who'd sacrificed everything to raise her little sister, never complaining when Emma got the best of everything. Paige had been proud that her hard work enabled Emma to have a normal life, that Emma was able to be a cheerleader and a homecoming queen and a beautiful, successful young woman with a bright future.

She had done that for Emma, and she'd been happy to do so.

But why did Emma have to get *everything?*

On the heels of jealousy, guilt rode hard. Who was Paige to deny her sister anything? Paige had been practically an adult when their mother died. Emma was the one who'd grown up without a loving mother. Paige had done everything for her, but a sister wasn't the same as a mother, no matter how hard she tried.

A tear spilled free, and then another, until finally Paige was curling her hands into Alexei's shirt as the first heartbroken sob escaped her. After that, it was easy to cry. She'd held the tears in for so long. She hadn't cried since her mother's funeral, had believed that tears made her weak.

Now, it felt good to let it all out. Cleansing. The man holding her never stopped rubbing her back, never made a move to pull away and leave her alone. Selfishly she clung to him and cried for all the years she'd lost.

While she cried herself out, she made a decision. From now on, Paige would no longer neglect her own happiness for that of others. When she wanted something, she would not deny herself. She was through denying herself.

It was a new day for Paige Barnes. And she knew just how to prove it.

CHAPTER THREE

ALEXEI SENSED THE change in her before she acted. One minute she was sobbing her heart out, the next she was standing on tiptoe and pulling him down for another kiss.

He was tempted. More than tempted. Alexei let her kiss him, fighting his reaction as her lips moved tentatively over his. She tasted like salt and sadness, and he wanted nothing more than to take that sadness away. It was his fatal flaw, this desire to protect and comfort those in need. He'd spent years fighting for his family, years that had taken their toll.

But there was nothing he could do for this woman. Though it would be so easy to take what she offered, so easy to sweep her into his arms and carry her to his room, he wasn't going to do it.

She wasn't kissing him because she wanted *him*. She was doing this to prove something to herself. And he didn't feel like being the conduit through which she tried to vanquish her anger and disappointment.

Her reaction to his news about her sister and Russell had not been what he'd expected. He'd set her up in his mind as a cold, calculating woman on a mission for her lover. He'd not stopped to think that maybe she really had been worried, or that she didn't know her sister wasn't missing but was instead sneaking off to Chad Russell's room.

Alexei didn't like the way her tears had made him feel, the

way her sweet vulnerability just now—the tentative kiss, the hint of desperation—struck a nerve inside him.

She brought memories crashing into his head that he tried to shove away. Memories of a pale, sad woman lying in a hospital bed, her lips cracked and dry, a lone tear sliding down her cheek as she whispered that she loved him.

The last person on this earth who loved him had died because he wasn't able to save her, because even though he was a prince, he'd been poor and broken and couldn't afford to buy the best leukemia treatments money could buy. After Katerina's death, he'd vowed on her memory that he would not be poor for the rest of his life. And he would strike back at the cold-blooded man who'd stripped them of everything before he'd returned to America with the rights to the land their mother had sold, and the rich oil and gas deposits beneath.

Tim Russell had left them with nothing, and though it would have taken only a fraction of the wealth he'd amassed from their land to help Katerina, he'd refused. Alexei had scraped together the money to fly to Dallas and beg for his sister's life, but he'd been met with cold disdain. He still remembered standing in Russell's office, high over the Dallas skyline, and being both awed and sickened by the wealth on display. He'd wanted that life for his family, and it had made him sick to think it might have been theirs had this man not stolen it from them.

Once Katerina had died, Alexei had found the initiative to start Voronov Exploration with nothing more than bravado and a geological engineering degree from Moscow University. He'd burned with a passion to regain everything that had been lost and to destroy the Russells in the process.

It had taken years, but he was at the pinnacle of his success now—and victory over the Russells was within his grasp. If he could turn back time, he would save his sister from the cancer that had eaten her strength and her life. He would give back all the money and give up the idea of vengeance if it was possible to have another chance.

But there was no going back. Ever. Life moved forward, no matter how much money you had. It hadn't helped Tim Russell when his time had come, and it wouldn't help his son when Alexei finally gained control of Russell Tech.

Alexei gripped Paige's arms, gently, and set her away from him. She sucked in a breath, and for a moment he thought she might start to cry again. Instead she wrapped her arms around her waist and stared up at him, her eyes huge pools of hurt.

He couldn't help but feel sympathy for her. Those tears had been real, regardless of her reasons for being here in the first place.

And maybe, just maybe, he could turn her anger and sadness at Chad Russell to his advantage. She was his secretary; she knew sensitive information about his business.

Information Alexei could use.

"You don't really want to do this," he said softly. "You are hurt and sad and you want to make it go away. I understand this. But tomorrow, you would have regrets."

She shrugged one shoulder, as if to say it mattered not at all to her. Yet he knew it mattered a great deal with that single movement.

"It's okay if you don't want to m-make love," she said, casting her eyes toward the floor when she said *make love,* as if it embarrassed her to say the words.

Now why did that hint of innocence spike the heat in his blood?

"Paige," he said, waiting until she looked at him again before he continued, "I think you need to get some sleep. Tomorrow, everything will look brighter."

How many times had he told that lie to Katerina? They'd

both known it was a lie, but it was a fiction they'd counted on to get them through the hard times.

"I have to be back at the hotel by eight," she said numbly. "Cha—my boss has an important meeting to attend."

Alexei couldn't stop himself from reaching out and tucking a wisp of hair behind her ear. He was the good guy here and he planned to make her see it. "*Da,* I know this."

She frowned. "I really wish you would tell me how you know these things."

He smiled as tenderly as he could. It was a risk, but if he wasn't truthful with her, she wouldn't trust him. And he wanted her trust now that Russell had broken it. It was vital to the new plan he was formulating.

"Because his meeting is with me."

Her eyes grew big. For the first time since he'd met her, he truly believed she had no idea who he was. His sense of purpose redoubled. He would destroy Russell Tech when he was through, thanks to this woman.

"You are Mr. Valishnikov?"

He shook his head. "I am the other V."

If anything, her eyes grew bigger. Her fingers flew to her mouth, pressed against her lips. When her hand dropped away, her face was pale.

"Oh my God," she said. "You're Prince Voronov."

It was snowing as the Mercedes moved through the city. Fat flakes that ghosted down and gathered on the pavement. Paige stared wide-eyed out the window. She'd never seen so much snow in her life, and it was April! Dallas was balmy this time of year, and Atkinsville, on the Gulf Coast where she'd grown up, had always been temperate.

She wanted to turn to the man sitting beside her, to thank him for taking her back to the hotel so early when the meeting wasn't for another two and a half hours, but she couldn't look at him.

Alexei Voronov. A *prince*. She'd been kissing a prince. Trying to seduce him when her feelings were hurt, and he'd turned her down flat. Of course he had! Not only was he a Russian prince, but he was also gorgeous on top of that. Not at all the sort of man to be interested in her.

Paige's face grew hot as she thought about how he'd kissed her in Red Square, the way his body ground against hers, the way she'd nearly splintered apart simply from the delicious pressure.

A game, she reminded herself. *A necessary act to save them both.*

But the man who'd rescued her wasn't just any prince. He was Prince Voronov—and Chad seemed to hate him. According to Chad, Prince Voronov was determined to absorb Russell Tech into his vast operations—which he would be in a prime position to do if he acquired Valishnikov's land.

If he succeeded in his quest, Russell Tech would cease to exist.

Jobs would be lost, people displaced—including herself. She wasn't unemployable, but in this current economic climate, how long would it take to find a new job? And how would she make her rent and utilities until then?

Worse, would she find new work in time to make Emma's tuition payment next semester?

Last night, she'd had plenty of time to think as she'd tossed and turned in the guest room Alexei had shown her to, and she'd realized that though she was hurt, it wasn't Emma's fault at all. Paige had never said she had a crush on Chad, and it wasn't fair to be mad at Emma. Her sister couldn't help being beautiful and vivacious; of course Chad had been attracted to her!

"You are very quiet, Paige."

She turned her head slowly, steeling herself to meet Alexei's gaze. Would she still see pity in his eyes? It was nothing but wishful thinking to hope he'd forgotten how she'd thrown herself at him after he'd told her about Chad and Emma. She wanted to sink into the leather cushions and disappear, but since that wasn't happening, she forced herself to be cool under pressure.

"I'm just thinking," she said. "We don't get snow in April where I'm from."

His smile made her heart thump. "Ah yes, it is quite tropical where you live."

"I wouldn't say tropical."

He shrugged. "Compared to Moscow?"

Paige swallowed. He was too handsome, this man. Too easy to look at. She found herself wondering what it would have been like if he hadn't pushed her away.

Mind-blowing, no doubt.

"I see your point."

"You should see my home in St. Petersburg," he continued. "It is an old estate dating back several hundred years in my family. The snow is pristine, undisturbed. There are wolves that howl during the night, and the stars shine so brightly you cannot believe. It is perfect for a *troika* ride."

She had a vision from a movie, of a couple bundled under a fur and riding through the snow in a sleigh with jingling bells. It seemed so romantic, though of course he hadn't mentioned it for that reason.

"That sounds lovely," she replied.

"Perhaps I will show it to you someday," he said, and her heart thumped harder.

Was he flirting with her?

Impossible. A man like him dated movie stars and models, not plain secretaries who were so pitiful they could only admire a man from afar.

"I don't see how," she replied truthfully, "though it's a nice thought. We are leaving in a few days, and St. Petersburg is not on our itinerary."

His gaze glittered strangely. "Do you intend to take your lover back after what he did?"

Shock zapped her like an electrical current. "Chad Russell is my boss, not my lover."

"Is that so?"

She thrust her chin forward. "Yes, it is."

He laced his fingers between hers, brought her hand to his mouth. She was too stunned to pull away as his lips touched the back of her hand. "Then that is really too bad for him, isn't it? But it's excellent for me."

When he released her, she clamped her hands together in her lap. Her skin still tingled from his touch. "I don't know why," she said as the blood roared in her ears. "You had your chance last night and you didn't take it."

Had she really just said that to him?

His laugh was not what she expected. "When I take you, *maya krasavitsa,* it will not be as you cry over another man."

Her face flamed. "I wasn't crying over Chad."

His expression said he didn't believe it. She turned her head to watch the snow again. Damn him for seeing so deeply into her. Her shattered romantic fantasy hadn't been the only thing she'd cried over, but she wasn't planning to share everything about her life with this man in order to correct his impression.

He was nothing to her, in spite of the heat of attraction she felt. After he dropped her off, she would never talk to him again.

"I think perhaps you are in love with Chad Russell," he said from behind her, "even if he is not your lover. And I think you are bitterly disappointed to learn he has chosen your sister over you."

Paige whirled, both stunned and furious. "You have no idea what you're talking about!"

"I am not a blind man, Paige."

Her breath stabbed in her chest. Was she that transparent? Had Chad always known it, too? Was that why he'd taken her to lunch? To try to let her down easily?

My God.

"Leave me alone, Prince Voronov," she said coldly. "I appreciate your help, but that doesn't give you the right to pick my life apart for your amusement. You don't know *anything* about me, so save your rude speculation."

The car drew to a halt, but she couldn't seem to look away from the man staring so intently back at her. His icy gray eyes weren't cold like she expected—they were hot, boring beneath her skin.

"Then I apologize," he said after what seemed an eternity of them staring at each other in silence. "I would never want to hurt you."

The door swung open and she realized they were at the hotel, that a valet waited for her to exit. But everything in the car was surreal, and she found it hard to break away. The next time she saw this man, it would be at a meeting of corporate bigwigs. He would not notice her—nor did she want him to.

If Chad knew she'd spent the night with Prince Alexei Voronov, even though it was innocent, he'd go through the roof.

And she'd definitely be out of a job.

"Thank you for your help," she said again. She felt like a broken recording, but what else could she say? Paige tried her best to smile as if she wasn't still raw inside. "I suppose this is goodbye then."

Alexei's smile was wolfish. "Ah, but this is not goodbye,

is it? We will see each other again, Paige Barnes. We will see
a lot of each other, I promise you."

Paige hurried from the car and dashed inside the hotel
lobby without looking back. Her skin was hot, in spite of the
frigid weather, and she stripped off her coat in the elevator
as it sped to her floor.

Why did Alexei Voronov rattle her so much? Yes, they'd
skipped a few steps with that meeting in Red Square, but a
kiss was a kiss. Wasn't it?

Paige's ears were hot. No, it definitely wasn't. That kiss
had been molten hot, and so had the kisses later, in his
apartment.

That didn't make the kisses extraordinary, however. And,
really, how would she know? She had very little to base it
on.

Paige fished her key from her coat and slipped into the
room she shared with Emma. A pang of feeling pierced her
heart, but she pushed it aside. So what if Emma was with
Chad? Paige was so over it.

"Oh my God, where have you been? I've been so
worried!"

Paige stopped dead in the midst of trying to close the door
silently, in case Emma was in bed after all, and turned very
slowly to face her sister.

Emma's pretty face was lined with worry. Paige's heart
squeezed in her chest.

"I'm sorry, Emma. I couldn't sleep and went for a walk."
The lie slipped from her tongue with ease, but guilt followed
in its wake. She didn't like lying to her sister, but it was easier
than explaining what had really happened.

And safer, too, since Emma could be a chatterbox. She
would innocently let slip the information that Paige had been
with the evil head of Voronov Exploration, and that would
be the end of Paige Barnes's career at Russell Tech. She'd be

on the next plane home with her tail tucked between her legs and no reference to find a new job.

She couldn't even think about the potential repercussions to Emma and her budding romance, if that's what it was, with Chad.

Emma tossed her glorious blond hair, her face shifting into a pout that Paige knew only too well. "You could have left a note."

"Why would I do that?" Paige asked. "You never wake up before eight anyway."

Emma had the grace to look sheepish. "Well, I did today. And you weren't here. I was about to call Chad to help me find you."

Déjà vu. Paige casually laid her coat over the back of the couch in their suite, thanking her lucky stars she'd returned when she did. The last thing she needed was Chad trying to find *her*.

"I'm here now, so you can stop worrying."

"You're wearing the same clothes as yesterday," Emma pointed out.

Paige felt her face grow hot. "I put them back on when I woke up. Now I'm going to shower and get ready for the meeting." She was almost to the bedroom door when she stopped and turned back. "You didn't come home last night, Emma. Where were *you?*"

Emma's face split into a grin. Typical of her sister that she wouldn't see a parallel between her actions and Paige's. It simply didn't occur to her that Paige might have panicked when *she* hadn't returned. She expected Paige to always be there for her, but she didn't seem to think it was a two-way street.

"I was with someone," Emma said. "And I think I'm in love."

Paige forced herself to remain calm even though her heart

was pounding a million miles an hour. "That's fast," she said. "You can hardly know this man."

"Oh, Paige," Emma said, her face glowing with happiness. "I wasn't going to tell you just yet, because I knew you'd worry, but it's Chad."

Paige blinked. "You're in love with Chad? But you barely know him—"

"I've been seeing him for a month."

Paige sank onto the closest chair. A month. One month of lies, obfuscations and going behind her back. No wonder Chad hadn't needed her to send flowers or make reservations.

And she was beginning to understand why he'd taken her for lunch.

"I had no idea," she said numbly.

Emma came over and knelt before her, took both of Paige's hands in her long-fingered elegant ones. "I'm sorry, but Chad thought you might be upset if you knew. We wanted to keep it a secret until we knew how we felt about each other."

Paige's hands were so cold inside Emma's warm ones. One sister had all the life and heat while the other was cold and empty. It didn't seem fair. "Isn't a month awfully quick to know if you love someone or not?"

Emma's smile said that it clearly was not. "Sometimes you just *know*."

In spite of her pain, it warmed Paige to see her sister so happy. She'd always wanted the best for Emma. Though there were only five years between them, she often felt more like Emma's mother than her sister.

But Emma's beatific smile worried her, too. Paige squeezed her hands. "I've worked for Chad Russell for two years, Emma. He dates a lot of women."

"I know that. But he loves me. He wants to marry me."

Her heart was splintering into a million jagged pieces around her. She hadn't realized until that moment that she'd been living for Emma. What would she do when Emma was gone?

And what should she say now? Emma was looking at her so hopefully, but all Paige could do was worry. Was Chad serious? Would he really put aside his playboy ways and make her sister happy? Or was he merely leading Emma along with no intention of marrying her? He was so rich. He moved in different social circles, circles that Emma had never been in before. Was this real, or was it simply another affair?

"Have you set a date?"

Emma shook her head as she stood. "When we get back to Dallas, we'll start discussing it. He's just so worried with this deal right now."

Paige's heart flipped. But whether it was from her misgivings about Chad's true intentions or about the deal that held Russell Tech's future in the balance, she wasn't sure. Because when she thought of the reason they were here in Moscow, she also thought of Alexei. He'd helped her when she needed it, held her while she cried, and kissed her so expertly that she'd practically begged him to take her to his bed—though of course she hadn't done it right since he had not complied.

But he wasn't just any man. He was Prince Voronov, and he was out to destroy Russell Tech. If he succeeded, then he also destroyed Chad and Emma's possibility of a happy future together.

Paige stood and hugged her sister tight. "I'm glad you're so happy and I hope Chad realizes how lucky he is to have you. Because if he doesn't," she continued, pushing Emma back to look at her, "I'll castrate him."

Emma laughed and hugged her back. "Don't worry about me," she said fiercely. "I'll do it myself if necessary."

"I have no doubt you will. And now," Paige said, "I need to get ready for this meeting."

As she stripped out of her clothes and stepped beneath

the shower, she couldn't shake a sense of impending doom. She was still reeling from Emma's news, and her heart still smarted, but that wasn't the problem at all.

No, it was Prince Voronov who spiked her anxiety. Because she'd realized in the car, when he'd seen through her masks, that he was a very dangerous man.

And not just to Russell Tech, but to her. In spite of her wish it were otherwise, her veins already bubbled in anticipation of seeing him again. The best thing he could do would be to ignore her.

But she knew he wouldn't do so. What she didn't know was why that knowledge made her happy.

CHAPTER FOUR

THE TENSION IN THE conference room wasn't surprising. But the tension coming from Paige Barnes was. Alexei watched her while Chad Russell spewed on and on in near flawless Russian. Since Paige didn't understand a word that was said until Chad turned and told her to write something down in English, she spent a lot of time staring at her lap.

Alexei willed her to look at him, but she did not. He hadn't been able to stop thinking about her since she'd dashed from his car this morning. She was an odd woman; beautiful, but completely unaware of her beauty.

And innocent. That's what compelled him. She reminded him of Katerina in a way. Katerina had only been seventeen when she'd died, and to the last she'd had that sweet air of innocence. Cancer and poverty had not been able to take it away.

Thinking of Katerina brought his gaze back to Chad Russell. It had been nearly fifteen years since Katerina's death. Chad could not be blamed for his father's cruelty, true, but Chad seemed to have shouldered the mantle of dislike his father'd had for the Voronov family. Alexei hadn't understood until that single moment so many years ago when he'd stood before Tim Russell why the man had hated them. And though he'd known it was likely Russell's son would follow in his father's footsteps, Alexei still found it difficult to believe.

Chad Russell was half Voronov, after all.

Still, it made what Alexei had to do that much easier. If Chad had been likable, or friendly in any way, Alexei might have let it color his desire to destroy Russell Tech. He glanced at Paige again. Regrettable that he would need to use her in his quest, but he would make sure she was handsomely rewarded in the end. He shoved away the twinge of conscience that threatened to badger him and focused on the discussion.

Alexei watched his first cousin gesticulate in an attempt to impress Valishnikov with his plans and ideas for the Siberian land and Baltic oil wells. Chad might be half Russian, but that wouldn't be enough to convince the old man sitting so stoically across the table. Though Chad's mother—Alexei's Aunt Elena—had clearly taught him the language, Chad's father had made certain his son was one hundred percent American.

And Pyotr Valishnikov was old enough to remember what it was like to hate and distrust Americans.

Worse, Chad looked every bit the American oilman stereotype. While he'd worn a dark suit, he also sported cowboy boots and a white Stetson that now sat on the table beside him. It was the wrong impression to make on this man.

Valishnikov raised his hand suddenly to indicate he wanted silence. Chad sputtered to a halt.

"I will consider your proposals," the old man said. "*Both* of your proposals. Now if you will excuse me, I have another meeting to attend."

He levered his bulk out of the chair and, followed by his contingent of managers and accountants, he exited the room.

Alexei noted Chad's reaction with interest. He seemed to fold in on himself, just for a moment, before shooting a glare at Alexei and squaring his jaw in a belligerent gesture.

"It seems as if you will be spending more time than you

bargained for in our fair country," Alexei said in English as he rose from his seat. "Perhaps you should take some time to sightsee. St. Petersburg is particularly lovely this time of year."

Just as he'd hoped, Paige's head snapped up. Her smoky eyes were huge in her face. Her glasses had fallen down the bridge of her nose and she pushed them back up with a finger.

He wanted to kiss the tip of that pert nose. The thought startled him. He could not afford to feel such romantic nonsense. She was a woman, an attractive woman, and she very possibly had information he needed. That was his sole reason for being interested in her.

"I'm not going to St. Petersburg, Prince Voronov." Chad sneered. "I'm staying right here until this deal is in the bag."

"You will not win."

Hatred oozed from the other man. "Don't be too sure of that." He turned to the woman sitting behind him. "Gather everything and meet me in the lobby. I have a phone call to make."

"Alone at last," Alexei said once Chad had stormed out of the conference room like a Texas whirlwind.

Paige crossed to the table, doing her best to give him the cold shoulder. "You shouldn't be talking to me," she said as she started to stack papers into neat piles. He did not miss that her fingers trembled.

"Why not? I like talking to you." Oddly enough, he truly did. He shouldn't, but she was refreshing in a way the women he usually dated were not. Still, he would not allow anything—not even her relative innocence—to interfere with his plan to ply her for information.

Her gaze snapped to his, then dropped again. A tinge of pink stained her cheeks. He liked that about her. Her long dark hair was gathered in a ponytail, and she wore a conservative black pantsuit with a high-collared white shirt. The suit fit her well enough, but she looked like a penguin.

A penguin he wanted to unwrap. She was too staid, too stuffy. It would be a pleasure to strip her of her businesslike formality, to see the sensual woman he'd glimpsed last night when he'd kissed her in the square. Her glasses slipped down her nose as she worked. She took a moment to shove them up again before continuing with her sorting.

"I work for Chad Russell," she said, "and I'd like to keep my job, if you don't mind. So please don't talk to me."

"Why is talking to you a bad thing?" he asked, moving around the table until he stood next to her. Until he could breathe in her summery scent.

Were those peaches he smelled? Unbidden, the thought she should be dressed in warm vibrant colors like summertime filtered into his mind. Though white suited her, like snow covering a pure landscape, it did not do so when overwhelmed by so much black.

So prim, this woman. She would be a challenge, perhaps. He liked challenges, relished them. Especially when they were unexpected.

She stopped what she was doing and turned toward him. He didn't miss the movement of her throat as she swallowed heavily. Her fingers shook where they rested on a pile of papers in midsort.

"Because I don't like lying to my boss, and because I don't want him to ask me anything about you—why I was talking to you, what I think of you—anything. Because talking to you tangles me in a web of lies, and I'm no good at it."

Alexei laid his hand over hers on the papers. He affected her. And he definitely planned to use it to his advantage, to romance her, to romance any information out of her that he could get. In war, he took no prisoners, eschewed no tactics.

He pushed aside a stab of guilt as he caressed the back of her hand. "Have dinner with me tonight."

Her jaw dropped. "Are you insane? Didn't you hear a thing I said? I can't have dinner with you!"

"Chad doesn't have to know," Alexei said, giving her hand a tug until she was flush against him. He had a sudden desperate urge to feel the warm softness of her body pressed against him again. To drown in her soft scent and softer skin.

When she tried to pull away, he tightened his grip.

"Let me go," she said quietly, her eyes downcast.

And though he didn't want to do it, though he wanted to kiss her into compliance, he did as she asked. She immediately stepped away and put her arms around her body.

Frustration sawed into him. "I admire your loyalty to your boss, Paige, but does he also command your personal life? Is he allowed to tell you whom you may or may not see?"

A shadow crossed her face. "Of course not. But this is complicated. You're the enemy."

Alexei couldn't contain a sharp laugh. He was indeed, but he didn't want her to think so.

"You *are*," she insisted, frowning. "To Chad, you are. And I work for him." She took a deep breath, let it out in a long sigh. "Besides that, he's asked my sister to marry him."

Alexei stopped laughing. Paige swiped a hand beneath her nose and turned to the papers once more. Clearly she was hurt by this new development. And he didn't like seeing her hurt. The change in her expression was like watching dark clouds blotting out the sun. It bothered him.

Watching her with Chad today, he could tell there was no relationship between them, no spark. It had made him absurdly happy. Yet now she was sad, and he didn't like it.

"I'm sorry, Paige."

She shrugged. "For what? This is a very good thing. My sister is very happy."

"Are you?"

Her shoulders seemed to slump. Just as quickly, she straightened and turned to look at him with pride on her face. "Yes, I am. Emma is beautiful and amazing and she deserves a man like Chad."

"And what do you deserve?"

Her lower lip trembled before her teeth stopped it. "I wish you wouldn't do that," she said very softly.

"Do what? I am asking you a question, such as one friend asks another."

"You aren't my friend."

He pressed his advantage. "Not yet. But I could be."

She shook her head. "Don't say things you don't mean, Prince Voronov. It's impossible, and you know it."

"Call me Alexei. And I can tell you what you deserve," he continued. He knew what she needed to hear. She was a woman who didn't believe in herself, and he was a man who was very good at saying the right things. She looked at him hopefully. He wondered if she knew she'd done so.

"You deserve to laugh," he said quietly, seriously. "You deserve to do something for yourself instead of always doing for others. You deserve happiness, Paige, and you deserve to stop worrying about everything and let someone else worry for you. You deserve flowers every day, candlelight dinners and a man who wants you very much. You deserve everything your sister has, and more."

Her eyes glistened. Her mouth dropped open, shut again, and he knew he'd hit the mark. Another spear of guilt shot through him. He didn't want to like her, didn't want to feel pleased that he'd moved her. He did what was necessary to avenge his family; he had no room for remorse.

"What makes you think I don't do anything for myself?

A few hours acquaintance hardly qualifies you as an expert on me."

She was defensive, and he didn't blame her. He'd gone deep and it had to sting.

"You are an open book, Paige Barnes. I am simply reading what is written for all to see."

Her dark eyes were wounded, as if he'd exposed the soft underbelly of her vulnerability with just a few words.

"I—I—" Whatever she was about to say was lost as her jaw snapped shut and she whirled away from him. Opening the briefcase, she shoved all the papers inside, no longer interested in order or neatness.

Alexei cursed inwardly as she jammed the lid shut and locked it. He'd gone too far, spooked her.

"I have to go," she said without looking at him again. "Chad's waiting for me."

Before he could stop her, she bolted from the room. For the second time today, Paige Barnes had run away from him.

Paige threw down her pen and pushed back from the desk in her room. How could she work when all she could think of was Alexei Voronov telling her she deserved happiness and love?

Of course he hadn't meant *he* was the man who was going to give her those things, but she'd felt as if she must look so pitifully grateful, so hopeful, that she'd reacted defensively. And when he'd called her an open book, it too eerily echoed her own thoughts. She'd suddenly felt the urgent need to escape before she embarrassed herself any further.

She was a strong woman. She'd been strong all her life, and she'd taken care of herself and her sister since their mother had died. She'd sacrificed and scraped, and she was independent and moderately successful. So why did she dissolve into a puddle of mush around a man she barely knew? Why did he make her feel so vulnerable?

A glance at her watch told her it was nearly four in the afternoon. It felt earlier since the sun usually set so late here in the spring and summer—though you wouldn't know it was spring with the snow outside. But her stomach growled and she realized she hadn't eaten since grabbing a pastry and coffee this morning before going to the meeting. She thought about ordering room service, but decided that going to the hotel restaurant was a better idea.

She'd locked herself inside since she'd returned a few hours ago, and it was time to get out, among people. Perhaps then she would stop thinking so much about one Russian prince.

Chad and Emma were off somewhere, and would be spending their free time together for the rest of the time they were here. Now that Paige knew about the relationship, there was no need to keep up the pretense. Chad had apologized to her on the ride to the meeting this morning. He'd wanted to tell her, he'd said, but he hadn't been sure she would approve.

She'd admitted that she wouldn't have, and—without a care for possible job ramifications—had told him that if he hurt her sister, she'd gut him. He hadn't fired her, as she'd half expected, but had instead assured her that he loved Emma and would never hurt her.

While they were at the meeting, Emma had moved her suitcases to Chad's room.

Which left Paige alone and feeling kind of blue. Though Emma was in college, she'd continued to live at home. Paige was accustomed to having someone there. Of course she'd taken business trips before, and of course she'd stayed alone. But this trip seemed so different, and Emma's absence so final, that it bothered her more than she'd thought it would.

Paige hadn't changed out of her suit earlier, so she grabbed her jacket and took the elevator down to the lobby. Fifteen minutes later, she was seated in a corner booth and contemplating the English menu a waiter had brought.

"Don't order the *borscht*," a deep voice said. Her head snapped up, her gaze colliding with icy gray eyes. Her pulse shot skyward.

He slid into the booth seat opposite her. "Everyone who comes to Russia orders *borscht*, but there is far more to our cuisine than cabbage."

"What are you doing here?" Paige demanded. "Go away before you get me in trouble!"

"Do not worry, Paige. No one will see you talking to me."

"You don't know that," she insisted. "What if Chad gets hungry? What if he comes in here?"

He shrugged. It infuriated her the way he so casually dismissed her fears. He was rich, and he didn't have to worry about losing his job. But she had so much more to worry about than her job now that Chad was planning to marry her sister. She would *not* cause problems between them.

"You should have agreed to come to dinner with me. Then we would not be here, but elsewhere."

Paige gritted her teeth. "Go away."

He leaned back against the cushions and shot her an arrogant grin. "Only if you go with me."

Her heart leaped into double time. "I'm not going with you, Alexei."

"Then I will stay with you," he said, reaching for the menu.

She held it tight, refusing to let go.

"This is a nice hotel," he said, "but it caters to tourists. Wouldn't you like to try real Russian food? See more than the inside of your room and the airport?"

"I've already been to Red Square," she said primly.

His grin could have melted an iceberg. "I have fond memories of your trip to Red Square."

Paige tried not to blush, though she could feel the heat creeping into her cheeks. For once in her life, she wished she'd slept around more. Then she wouldn't be so affected by Alexei Voronov's wicked grin.

"You didn't really come here to make me go to dinner with you," she said, trying to interject some reality back into the situation.

"No. I had to meet with someone. But I saw you enter the restaurant, and I couldn't pass up the opportunity to see you again."

"Stop saying things like that."

"Why not? You are a beautiful woman, and I wanted to see you."

No one had ever called her beautiful. She was passably pretty, but she was too plain to be beautiful. Fashion confused her, makeup was a mystery that she'd only partially solved—blush, lipgloss and mascara usage were pretty simple—and her hair was so long and thick that she usually just ended up with a ponytail. Emma tried to get her to wear trendier clothes, but she never felt quite right in them. Emma's style was wrong for Paige, and since she didn't really know how to find her own, she settled for business suits and jeans. It was a safe wardrobe. Conservative.

"I can see you do not believe me," Alexei continued. "This shocks me, Paige."

She lifted her chin a notch while she clutched the menu between her hands. "I don't trust you, Prince Voronov. You have an ulterior motive."

His face split into another of those jaw-dropping grins. "How well you know me already," he purred. "I do have an ulterior motive." Then he leaned forward and caught one of her hands in his. "The motive is that I want you to come with me now. I promise Chad will never know. He may speak Russian, but he does not know this place like I do. He will not venture beyond the more trendy districts."

"And you want to take me somewhere that isn't trendy?" She pulled her hand away, though her heart continued to beat overtime. "I'm not sure if I should be insulted or relieved."

Oh my God, she was bantering with him.

His sensual mouth curved, showing impossibly white teeth. "I would take you to the finest restaurant in the city, if you would allow me. But since you will not, I want to take you somewhere even better."

"Better than the finest restaurant in the city? That doesn't seem possible, now does it?"

"It is very possible, I assure you. You have only to say yes, and you will find out. Come with me now, Paige."

She liked talking to him. He took away the loneliness, and he made her insides churn with excitement. Warmth flowed through her like she'd submerged in a hot bath. It made her languid and less uncertain.

Was it truly wrong to consider going to dinner with him? Chad and Emma were very likely locked in their suite, ordering room service and making love. Why couldn't she see the city and enjoy herself for a while? What was the harm in that?

"I can't," she said, a hint of desperation creeping into her voice. Because she wanted to go. She wanted to spend more time with this man who told her she was beautiful. He made her feel like she was someone special, even if it were an illusion. It was a new feeling and she liked it way too much.

"That is Chad Russell talking," he said disdainfully. "I want to hear what Paige Barnes wants."

Paige closed her eyes. She wanted to see the city, and she wanted to have dinner with a handsome man who gave her compliments. "It's too complicated. I shouldn't go."

"What is complicated about eating together?"

But why couldn't she have an evening of fun? Emma was with Chad, and they were so happy with each other that they wouldn't notice if Paige went out for a few hours. So long as the restaurant was far from the hotel and not a place likely to be frequented by tourists, what was the harm? She'd already spent the night with this man. It couldn't get any worse than that.

Besides, what had happened to her vow to live for herself, to do what Paige wanted for a change?

"Yes," she breathed before she could change her mind. "I'll go to dinner with you."

"Speciba," Alexei said as he slid from the seat and grabbed her hand. He tossed some bills down on the table, though she'd ordered nothing yet, and tugged her toward the exit.

"Wait, I need my coat," she said, pulling against him. She hadn't expected them to move so fast once she'd agreed. She'd thought she would have time to run up to her room and get her coat at the very least.

"I will buy you a coat," he replied.

"I can't let you do that."

"Of course you can." He dragged her into one of the shops in the lobby, picked out a long white coat made of the finest cashmere and wrapped her in it while the shopgirl oohed and ahhed.

"Alexei—"

"Quiet, Paige."

Next he selected a fur cap, like the one he'd worn last night, though in white, a snowy scarf and matching gloves made of the finest kid. Then he took a credit card from the breast pocket of his jacket and handed it to the cashier before Paige could insist on paying for it herself.

A moment later and he was hustling her out the lobby doors and into a long black limousine.

"I want to pay you for everything," she said as the car started to roll down the driveway.

"I will not take your money. Consider it a gift."

"I insist, Alexei." She folded her arms and stared at him, daring him to argue. How could she accept a gift so fine? She could not be indebted to him. Dinner was one thing, but a cashmere coat that must have cost at least five hundred dollars?

"Very well," he said easily. "We will set up a payment plan. One hundred of your U.S. dollars a month for the next sixty months…"

Paige blinked. "Six thousand dollars? You spent six thousand dollars?"

He reached out and tipped a finger under her chin. Her mouth snapped closed as she realized her jaw had been hanging open.

"*Da,* but you needed a coat."

She started to shrug out of the garment, but he stopped her.

"Don't be a fool, Paige. It pleases me to buy this for you. You do not need to pay me."

She looked away as, ridiculously, her eyes filled with tears. When was the last time she'd gotten a gift for no reason whatsoever? Not since before her mother died. Mama had loved surprising her daughters with small trinkets—until she had the accident and every penny they had went toward her care.

Paige couldn't accept such an extravagant gift from this man. It wasn't right. "I'll give everything back when you return me to the hotel."

Alexei swore in Russian. Or so she assumed by the expression on his face. "Very well," he said, stony-faced. "Whatever pleases you, Paige Barnes."

And now she felt ungrateful. She'd hurt his feelings, and it bothered her. She was Southern—and like all Southern women, she'd been inculcated with graciousness and sensitivity to others' feelings from birth. She'd failed miserably just now.

Paige touched his sleeve. "Thank you for the coat, Alexei. It was kind of you."

He swung around to look at her, his brows drawn down over his remarkable eyes. Why did he have to be so breathtaking?

"I do not understand you, Paige."

She blew out a breath. The air in the car was warm, and she was feeling toasty and comfortable. "I'm not sure I understand myself," she said with a shaky smile. "But I'm sorry I was rude."

He waved a hand, as if dismissing the last few minutes from his mind. "And I am sorry if I made you uncomfortable. It was not my intention."

Paige's gaze dropped. She twisted her fingers together in her lap. "I have to admit I'm uncomfortable simply being with you," she said. "I don't want to cause any trouble."

"There will be no trouble."

"If I were your employee, and you saw me with Chad, would you be angry?"

"Truthfully? Yes. But," he said before she could interject anything, "I would not fire you simply because of that. Far better to keep you close."

She frowned. "Really? Why?"

He leaned in as if he were imparting a secret. "Because you might know things that could be valuable to my enemies."

Her stomach bottomed out. "You'd be mistaken," she said softly. "I don't know anything. And even if I did, I wouldn't tell you. If that's why you've gone to all this trouble, you're wasting your time."

Alexei grinned, and her insides melted in spite of her wish

not to react. "Such a little *teegr,* Paige. This is why I like you. You are loyal, even when he has hurt you deeply."

She twisted her fingers together in her lap. "I'm not hurt. I was simply surprised. And concerned for my sister."

"Your sister is old enough to take care of herself, don't you think?"

Paige frowned. He didn't understand, and she couldn't really explain it. "That's not the point. I feel responsible for her, and I love her. I won't let anyone hurt her."

"Of course you love her," he said. "But you are not responsible for her."

"You don't know anything about us," she protested. "It's easy for you to sit there and pronounce judgment, but until you've walked a mile in my shoes, you have no right to tell me how to feel."

He took one of her hands in his, rubbed stomach-flipping circles in her palm. "I am not telling you how to feel. But a twenty-one-year-old makes her own decisions. You are not responsible for what she chooses."

Her breath left her on a long sigh. "I know. But you don't stop worrying about someone just because they become an adult. I raised Emma. In some ways, she's like my child."

She'd never said that aloud to anyone, she realized. It was shocking to voice it to this man she barely knew. Of course people back in Atkinsville knew she'd raised Emma after their mother's death, but Paige had never told anyone how truly hard it had been. To open up would have been to admit she needed help—which might have led to Child Services intervening.

"Ah, Paige, this makes so much sense now."

"What makes sense?" The circles in her palm continued. Her body was softening, melting, her core liquefying beneath his touch. My God.

"Why you feel so responsible, why you would sacrifice your own happiness for hers."

"I didn't say that. Emma doesn't need me to be unhappy just so she can be happy."

His eyes were sympathetic, understanding. "You must have been very young when you had to become her mother."

"Eighteen," she said.

"It was difficult for you, yes?"

Paige sighed. Why was she telling him this? And yet it felt somewhat comforting to do so. Like her tears the other night, it was cleansing to finally let it out. "Of course. I was still a kid myself and I didn't always know what to do. I didn't get everything right."

"Yet you did enough. She is grown and independent. You must allow her to sink or swim on her own."

"I appreciate what you're saying, but you have no idea—"

"I had a sister," he said very suddenly, his eyes shadowed. "She was three years younger than I. I protected her fiercely, Paige. But I could not save her in the end. I only wish she'd lived long enough to be able to drive me insane with her choices." He squeezed her hand then. "Celebrate your sister's ability to do so, and stand by her when she falls—but do not ever feel as if you must cease to live your life in order to always be there for her."

Paige couldn't speak. Shock—and fear—had frozen her vocal cords. How did he see inside her like this? How did he *know* what her fears were, and what she'd given up over the years without her actually telling him the details? It was disconcerting.

And yet she also ached for him. For the loss that clearly still affected him. She wanted to say she was sorry, wanted to ask what had happened, but before she could find her voice again, his phone rang.

"You will please excuse me, I must take this," he said, frowning at the display. Paige nodded—but she needn't have bothered because he was already talking.

He spent the next thirty minutes on the phone as the car glided through the city. The farther they drove from the hotel, the more Paige started to wonder if she'd made a mistake. She usually deliberated before she made decisions. She did not act on impulse.

Until now.

She'd signed on for a nice, authentic dinner in a real Russian restaurant with a man who fascinated her. She'd not expected to have her soul bared to him, or to experience the chink in her heart when she'd realized he'd also lost someone he loved.

It was supposed to be *dinner.* Nice, simple, easy.

But the car kept moving farther and farther from the city center. They passed from the densely packed buildings of Moscow into the outskirts before rolling along a congested highway. She wanted to ask Alexei where they were, but he was still on the phone.

When they took an exit and made a turn, she suddenly realized they were approaching an airport. Her stomach dropped to her toes. Though it didn't look like the same airport she'd flown into only a couple of days ago, it was still a large facility with a lot of traffic.

"It is *Sheremetyevo,*" Alexei said, as if he'd been reading her mind. He tucked his phone away. "You probably flew into *Domodedovo,* which is south of the city."

Paige tried not to panic. "Yes, but what are we doing here?"

"I am taking you to dinner, *maya krasavitsa.*" His expression said it was obvious.

"At the airport?"

"No," he said as the car hesitated for a moment at a security gate. The chauffeur exchanged a few words with the guards, and then they were through. A couple of minutes later the car came to a halt. The door opened and Alexei stepped out, then held out a hand for her. When she emerged, she realized they were standing in front of a hangar where a jet was slowly taxiing out into the open. The whine of the engines was loud, the wind whipping her clothes and making her wish she'd changed into jeans and boots instead of her business suit and kitten heels. In spite of the gorgeous coat, the wind went up her pant legs and chilled her from the inside out.

Alexei leaned into the car and grabbed the shopping bag with the accessories.

"Alexei," she shouted over the noise as he placed the hat on her head and wrapped the scarf around her neck, "I can't get on an airplane with you! This is insane!"

He didn't let go of her hand, instead tugging her into the curve of his body and wrapping an arm around her to keep her from getting too chilled.

"It is a short flight, Paige. I'll have you back by midnight, I promise. Put these in your pockets," he said, handing her the gloves.

Her pulse skidded like an out of control ice skater. What had she gotten herself into? Agreeing to go to a restaurant with him was one thing, but getting onto a plane?

"I can't," she said, shaking her head frantically. They both knew she wasn't talking about the gloves.

He turned her and put both hands on her shoulders. Then he leaned down until his face was only inches from hers.

"You trusted me last night," he said, his voice soothing in spite of the fact he had to practically shout. "I'm asking you to trust me again."

CHAPTER FIVE

HE WOULDN'T TELL HER where they were going, yet she'd still gotten onto the plane with him. Paige shook her head at her own folly, wondering what on earth had happened to her good sense. It had taken less than an hour for the plane to land at a different airport, but instead of getting into a car, they'd boarded a helicopter.

It wasn't her first helicopter ride, but it was certainly the most luxurious. The inside of the craft looked like a custom yacht, all white leather and sleek wood. Beside her, Alexei was on the phone. He'd taken at least six calls since she'd climbed into the car with him outside the hotel.

But then, that's what multimillionaire—or billionaire— tycoons did. They made deals over the phone, bought and sold entire companies and transferred millions of dollars, or rubles as the case may be, with aplomb.

It was a world far outside her realm, in spite of the last few days as Chad's executive secretary.

Alexei tucked the phone back into his pocket. "I am sorry for the interruptions," he said.

Paige shrugged. "It's okay," she replied. "There's a lot at stake."

His gaze sharpened as he studied her. "Yes, there is. And I intend to win, Paige."

A shiver skidded through her. She hadn't been referring to

any one deal in particular, but clearly the Valishnikov acquisition was the subject of his many calls. Apprehension was a tight ball in her stomach as she thought of her boss back in Moscow. "So does Chad."

He looked out the window behind her as the helicopter began to bank. "Look."

She turned to where he'd pointed, her breath catching in her throat. She felt him move behind her on the luxurious leather bench, felt his solid body pressing against hers. It was intimate, casual, but she burned nonetheless.

Below, the land unfolded itself in a crystalline white blanket. A rich green and white palace sat in the center of the covering. Six massive white columns fronted the building, and ornate friezes clad in gold surrounded each of the myriad windows across the three-level facing. The domes of a small church nearby were a muted gold, though she imagined they would glint in the sun, while white trees reached with bare arms to the dull sky.

Alexei's arm was on her shoulder, his cheek near her other ear as he leaned in and pointed. "It is the Voronov Palace," he said, "built in the early eighteenth century. Look there, at the fountain. It was a gift from Tsar Peter the Great."

The fountain in the front courtyard seemed made of gold, its cherubs and mythical creatures frozen in time, waiting for some sign only they knew in order to step down from their perches and frolic in the courtyard.

The Voronov Palace was fairy tale beautiful, and she felt completely out of her depth being here. She'd been raised in a two-bedroom house with a tiny kitchen and a postage-stamp lawn. Hardly comparable.

The helicopter made another pass, then began to hover before gliding softly down, its rotors lessening in speed until they were on the ground and a man opened the door and smiled at them. He said something in Russian. Alexei answered before turning and taking her hand in his.

Then they were stepping out of the craft and hurrying along a path that had been cleared of snow until they reached the house. Alexei led her inside a grand entry where Paige came to an abrupt stop, her head tilting back and her jaw dropping open.

The entry was vast, its gilt and alabaster walls rising to a dome that was painted all around with a scene from the bible. Three large crystal chandeliers were suspended from different points of the dome. The glittering crystals threw light into every nook and corner of the fresco, which gleamed with rich golds, deep blues, and vibrant reds.

"It's the Adoration of the Madonna," she said in wonder. Mama'd had a print of a religious scene similar to this one on the wall in their living room. Paige had been so accustomed to it that she'd lost the ability to see it with fresh eyes when she was still quite young.

But this was like seeing it again for the first time—though clearly this painting was far better. Not to mention *real*. Still, odd as it seemed, it gave her that wistful feeling of home.

"Da."

She looked at Alexei, blinking back tears. For a moment, she'd forgotten he was there. What must it be like to live with this kind of beauty every day of your life?

He came to her, his gaze filled with concern. "What is wrong, Paige? You are safe with me, I promise you."

It was too late to hide her reaction now. She gave him a watery smile, embarrassment creeping through her. "It's silly," she said, swiping her fingers beneath her eyes. "I always cry in art galleries. There's just something about the ethereal beauty of old paintings that gets to me. It's like the painter's soul is inside, if that makes sense. It's just so wondrous."

It was true, and yet she knew it was more than the beauty

of this painting making her cry. It was that connection to the past, discovered in such an unusual place, that made her more emotional than she might have otherwise been.

Alexei wiped away a tear that slipped down her cheek. His handsome face was gentler than she'd ever seen it. "You are very refreshing, Paige Barnes. I do not think I've ever met a woman who cries in art galleries, though this is hardly a gallery."

She managed a soft laugh. Hardly a gallery? Who was he kidding? "Well, I've only been inside three in my life, not including this place, so maybe it's not a phenomenon so much as the newness of the experience. I might grow positively callous with time."

He smiled. "I doubt that. And I think I had better not take you into the portrait gallery. You'll never be able to eat dinner with your nose closed from crying."

"Maybe after dinner then?" How could she not want to see portraits of his ancestors?

"After dinner is a surprise." He took her hand and pulled her to his side. "Now come, if I'm not mistaken, a delicious meal awaits us in the library."

"The library?" she said as they moved deeper into the house.

"The formal dining room is vast, whereas the library is far more cozy."

If cozy was a two-story room the size of a small department store, then yes, this room was cozy, Paige thought, as Alexei ushered her into a book-lined space with a giant fireplace burning at one end. A round table was set near the fire with crystal, china and snowy-white linens. A trio of uniformed servants stood to one side, near a cart from which glorious smells wafted.

Alexei took her coat and hat and handed them to one of the servants. Then he piled his own on top and came to pull out a chair for her. Paige sank into the worn leather, wondering how many Voronov princes and princesses had used this very chair she was sitting on.

Alexei took the chair opposite, and the food began to arrive. There were meat dishes, steamy dumplings, fragrant vegetables and black bread. A dish of black caviar in ice sat to one side, along with flat pancakes she knew were called *blini*. One of the servants opened a bottle of white wine and poured it into their glasses. Paige started to ask for water as well, but Alexei said something in Russian and a glass of water appeared at her place setting immediately after.

The waiters filtered out of the room and they were suddenly alone. Alexei lifted his wineglass. "To a fine evening of good food and great company."

Paige clinked glasses with him. She took a small sip of the wine, surprised to find it light and refreshing, and smiled back at him. Her pulse thrummed, and she wondered how she would get through this evening when suddenly she couldn't think of a single thing to say.

It was completely unreal, what was happening to her. She'd been whisked away from Moscow by a Russian prince, flown on his private plane to St. Petersburg and now she was sitting in the beautiful library of his ancestral home and eating a romantic dinner with him. These things happened in movies, or to beautiful models and actresses, but not to hardworking career women like her.

She thought of Chad and Emma, and pushed away a spear of guilt that notched into her breastbone.

"You are enjoying the *pelmeni?*" Alexei asked.

"Everything is wonderful. But which dish is *pelmeni?*"

"The dumplings. The filling is a mixture of beef, lamb, pork and spices."

Paige stabbed another. "It tastes amazing. You were right there's more to Russian food than cabbage."

He followed the fork from her plate to her mouth, his gaze lingering while she chewed. She was beginning to feel self-conscious, but then he looked down at his own plate and resumed eating.

"They were my sister's favorite," he said. "It is a recipe from the Urals. My mother made them for us quite often."

"I'm sorry that your sister is no longer with you," she said carefully. And then she wanted to smack herself. Could she have sounded any stiffer? Any more uncomfortable?

"It has been many, many years," he replied. "But thank you."

When he didn't say anything else, she felt duty-bound to change the subject. Another tenet of the Southern creed: *never make folks uncomfortable, and never talk about upsetting subjects.*

"My mother cooked a mean Southern-fried chicken," she said lightly. "That was my favorite growing up."

He looked at her with interest. "But not any longer?"

Paige shook her head. "Not since I learned about cholesterol and heart disease. And not since I lost ten pounds once I gave up fried foods."

Though she'd probably still be eating Mama's chicken if Mama were alive to make it.

"I have never had this Southern-fried chicken before."

"If you ever come to Texas, I'll make it for you." Polite chitchat was the hallmark of Southern manners. She didn't expect he would truly come, but she felt obligated to say it.

He grinned. "Perhaps I will plan a visit."

Paige took another sip of her wine. After tonight, the last thing she needed was for this man to come to Texas and see her meager little house. Nor was he likely to do so, really. He was simply being polite in return.

"Your home is lovely," she said. "It must have been amazing growing up here."

His expression clouded, but then he shrugged. "I did not grow up here, *maya krasavitsa*. My father died when I was five, and my mother was forced to leave with my sister and me. We were, as you say, persona non grata."

She felt she should drop it, and yet she found she could not. "That seems so unfair. Shouldn't your mother have inherited the property when your father died?"

He took a sip of his wine. "You would think so, but no. Times were hard back then, and Mama did not have, shall we say, the right connections. There were those who very much wanted her gone."

"But you are here now," she said, trying to recover from her mistake.

"It took many years, but yes, I managed to buy the property back." His ice-gray eyes glittered with an emotion she could not identify. Hate? Rage? Fear?

Before she could figure it out, his mask slipped back into place. Once more he was the handsome, solicitous Russian prince.

She stabbed her fork into a pile of greens. "Where does your mother live now?"

The seriousness never left his expression. She began to get a bad feeling that she'd somehow blundered again.

"She is in the church you saw when we arrived. As are my sister and my father. I moved my mother and sister here to join him when I took possession."

Paige felt her stomach drop. She set the fork down. He'd gotten the family home back, but his family wasn't here to enjoy it with him. "I'm so sorry, Alexei. I shouldn't have asked—"

"How could you know?" He reached for her hand across the table. "They have all been gone a very long time now. But they are where they should be, in the family crypt, and I am happy I could give that to them."

She squeezed his hand, her heart going out to him. Though it was no consolation, she wanted him to know that she understood. "My mother died eight years ago."

"I am very sorry for your loss."

She shook her head. She was messing everything up, failing in her efforts to comfort him. Turning the conversation to oneself at a time like this was unforgivably rude—and not at all what she'd intended. "I didn't tell you because I wanted sympathy. I just wanted you to know that I understood what it's like to be alone."

He looked surprised, but he quickly hid it. "You have Emma."

She swallowed. "Yes, but not for much longer."

He lifted her hand and kissed it. "You will always have her, Paige. She is still your sister."

Paige's throat felt tight. He'd lost his sister, and she was complaining about hers moving out and getting married? What was wrong with her? "Goodness, how did we end up talking about me when we were talking about you?"

"I like learning about you," he said.

"I'd rather talk about you."

"What do you wish to know?" he asked, leaning back in his chair. His black hair gleamed in the firelight as he focused on her. Her thoughts began to stray, but the hint of a grin on his face brought her back to the present.

Paige's pulse ticked up. There was one thing she wanted to know most of all, but she hardly dared ask. Then again, why shouldn't she? She'd already strayed outside the bounds of polite conversation. "Why are you being so nice to me, Alexei?"

If she thought he would be put off guard by her question, she was wrong. He smiled lazily, his gaze glittering as he looked at her. "You have to ask after last night?"

She wanted to believe him, but she was too practical to do so.

"If you want information, you're wasting your time. Until this trip, I was a junior secretary. Chad only picked me to come because of my sister."

Saying it aloud hurt, but it was the truth. Chad had chosen her for this trip because of Emma. Because they didn't want to be apart, and without Mavis, he needed a secretary anyway. It had been the perfect cover. It was embarrassing to admit to anyone, much less to a man as successful as Alexei Voronov.

But she would not have him believe she knew things she did not. If he took her back to Moscow right this instant, then so be it. At least she would know what his true motive had been.

"Does that anger you?"

His question took her by surprise. It wasn't what she'd expected out of him, but she decided to answer honestly. "Yes, but that's life, isn't it? I'm still good at what I do, and this trip is still an opportunity. Provided you don't acquire the land and close Russell Tech for good."

He looked very dark, very dangerous in that moment—as if his masks had all been stripped away and only the essence remained. A dark, cold, cruel essence.

"*When* I win, I will not close Russell Tech," he said. "I will absorb it."

Her temples throbbed with the beginnings of a headache, and she felt hot in her itchy wool-blend suit. *You started it,* she reminded herself.

"Chad says you would destroy the company and we'd all be out of work."

Alexei made a noise. "Chad is wrong. Though there will be some reorganizing, you would still have a job, Paige.

You would simply be working for me instead of for Chad Russell."

It was his cold certainty, his arrogant assumption about her that made her say what she did next.

"*If* you win, I'll look for another job."

How could he imagine she would want to work for him? It wasn't because of the animosity between him and Chad, or the repercussions to Russell Tech, though of course those things bothered her.

No, it was because of this, tonight. Because he gave every appearance of liking her and then spoke of her working for him as if tonight had never happened.

But what has *happened, Paige?*

Aside from the extravagance of his method, he'd done nothing more than take her to dinner. Yes, he'd kissed her last night, but she didn't fool herself it'd meant anything. Everything about last night had been outside the realm of normal, from the kiss in Red Square to the kisses in his apartment later.

"Why would you not want to work for me?" he demanded.

She laid her napkin on the table, her appetite gone. There was another reason, a more important reason than her wounded pride. And she had no problem telling him what it was.

"If you ruin Chad, then you ruin my sister's happiness. I can't work for the man who hurts Emma. She's done nothing to deserve it."

Alexei could only stare. She bristled like a wild Siberian tiger, her eyes sparkling in challenge, her creamy skin golden in the firelight. He should tell her she was foolish, but instead he wanted to drag her into his arms and kiss her.

No, he wanted to do more than that. He wanted to strip that ugly suit from her body and bury himself inside her. The urge was overwhelming, surprising.

Alexei stood abruptly, before he acted upon his impulse. She tilted her head back, a shadow of alarm crossing her features before she veiled it.

It bothered him, the way she sometimes looked at him like he was a great Russian bear planning to devour her whole. Like he was a character in a Dostoevsky novel, a human personification of impartial evil.

Perhaps he was.

But he had reason. And he would not crumble now, not when victory was so close. Not when she was here, and he wanted her. He'd told himself he wanted to find out what she knew about Chad's business, but he was beginning to believe the truth was a bit more complicated.

That his need for her was based on more than expedience.

He wanted her, but he hadn't expected to like her. She'd surprised him with how interesting she truly was. She was a woman who appreciated beauty so deeply it made her cry, and who protected her sister with a fierceness he could well understand. And she was loyal, steadfastly so, in spite of the insult she'd been dealt by the two people she'd come to Russia with.

He tried not to think of what he planned to do as yet another betrayal of her trust when she'd already suffered so many. He did what he must.

It was *necessary*. Some promises went deeper than any misgivings he might have. Her sister might be hurt if Chad lost his business, but she would recover. And Paige would recover as well. This was not a life or death situation.

He had to be ruthless. He was too close to his goals not to be. Katerina deserved it. His mother deserved it. Tim Russell had cost them everything, and Alexei wouldn't be finished until he'd stripped everything from Tim's son and wife.

He would not allow this one intriguing woman to divert his focus.

"Nevertheless, you will have a job should you want it. Now come," he said, offering her his hand as he shoved away any thoughts of taking her back to Moscow immediately. "This is no time to talk about business."

"Where are we going?"

"It is a surprise."

She still glared at him, her color high in her cheeks, but he held his hand steady and waited. He didn't think she would accept, but then she sighed and placed her small hand in his. The touch of her skin sent a shock of desire coursing through him. He tried to push it away, but the feeling was too strong.

A shudder rippled down his spine. He could not let her go now even if he wanted to.

She rose in a fluid movement to stand at his side. He was hyperaware of her, could feel her breath ghosting in and out of her lungs, her blood flowing through her veins, her answering desire thickening and burgeoning inside her body.

Her color was still high, but he knew it was for a different reason now. It gratified him, this knowledge that she wanted him, even while it made him feel as if he were imprisoned behind bars—because he could not act on it, not yet.

But he would as soon as the moment was right.

Instead he drew her to the window and stepped back so she could see. Outside, in the snow that was beginning to sparkle as the sun sank beneath the cloud cover and shot its last rays over the icy landscape, three horses were hitched side by side to a *troika*. A groomsman stood at their heads, holding them in place, while another checked the traces on the sled.

He heard the intake of her breath, the little gasp of wonder, and he took advantage of her change in mood to press in closer. To settle his hands on her shoulders and lean down to nuzzle her ear.

"As promised," he whispered, his lips finding and nibbling her tender earlobe. He allowed himself that much because he could not stop. Soon, very soon, he would take her to his bed.

Her only answer was a shudder.

CHAPTER SIX

THE AIR SMELLED CRISP and clean, and Paige couldn't help but laugh as the *troika* glided over the snow. The horses snorted and tossed their heads, the bells and tassels shaking with their movements as Alexei drove them down a lane beneath trees covered in white.

"It's glorious," she said. "Thank you so much."

"It would be a shame to come all this way and not experience it, *da?*"

She was bundled in her new coat, with the fur hat pulled down over her head and tickling her skin where it touched. She was warm, and yet a shiver of excitement arced over her body. Paige pulled the thick blanket that lay across their legs higher.

"Are you cold?"

"Not at all," she replied.

He looked concerned. "If you are cold, we will return to the palace. You have only to say so."

Paige touched his sleeve. "Not yet, Alexei," she said. "I don't want it to end so soon."

He smiled down at her. "Then we will keep going."

Truthfully, once he'd stood up from the table, she'd thought the evening was over. And she'd believed it was probably best that way, no matter how her heart pinched at the thought.

Because what on earth was she doing? This man was a

prince, he lived in a palace and he was trying to destroy her boss's—soon to be brother-in-law's—company. She had no business being here, no business enjoying her time with him.

It was wrong.

Yet here she was, sitting beside him in a sleigh, gliding across a darkening landscape that was lit by the fat moon hanging low in the sky. The cloud cover of earlier hadn't dissipated, but it had lessened enough that the moon shone brightly so long as it was close to the horizon. Another couple of hours, and the light would be gone as the moon rose into the high clouds.

It was romantic, being out here like this, something she would remember for as long as she lived. She did not regret this moment, even if she felt guilty for enjoying it.

After a few minutes more, Alexei pulled the horses to a stop in a clearing on a small rise.

"If the weather were normal for this time of year, we wouldn't be able to do this," he said to her. "But we had a late snowstorm."

"I'm glad it snowed," she replied, smiling up at him.

He touched a gloved hand to her cheek. She shivered, but not from cold. No, when Alexei touched her, it was like a furnace fired up in her belly. Every part of her felt hot. She remembered his lips on her ear, and her skin glowed. She'd almost turned in his arms, almost told him to forget the *troika* and take her to bed instead.

Fortunately she'd shocked herself so much with the idea that she had not acted upon it.

"Perhaps the snow came for you," he said softly.

A blast of heat sizzled through her core. Any second, she'd need to rip off her coat and hat and let the frigid air chill her skin. He leaned toward her, his head dipping lower. She was wrong to want him, and yet everything about this moment was magical.

She stretched up to meet him—

And gasped as a mournful howl split the night.

"Wolves," Alexei said. "There aren't as many as there used to be, but they still come at night."

"Shouldn't we go?" Another howl sounded in the distance and one of the horses snorted. Bells tinkled musically.

"There is nothing to fear. We are not too far from the palace, and I am armed."

Paige squinted into the remote landscape. The snow went as far as the eye could see, but no shapes moved upon it. Still, the animals were close. "They sound hungry."

"Yes, but there is prey here. Wild boar and goats will feed their bellies."

"I'm not certain I find that reassuring." She looked up to find him watching her with an odd expression. "What is it, Alexei?"

"You look as if you belong here," he said. "I knew white would suit you instead of black. The coat, the hat. Your cheeks are red, your eyes bright and your lips…" His gaze dropped to her mouth. "Your lips need kissing."

"Alexei," she began. The rest was lost as his mouth came down on hers.

She knew she should stop him, but she simply wasn't capable of it. She *wanted* his kiss, wanted his touch. He groaned low in his throat as their tongues tangled. One arm came around her, pulled her in close, while his other held the reins. Paige grasped his lapels, tilted her head back as she pressed herself closer to him.

She let him pillage her mouth, her heart pounding so hard in her chest she was certain he could feel it. This was the kiss in the square, but bumped up a few thousand degrees. She felt as if she'd known him forever, as if she'd been destined to arrive at this very moment *forever.*

Everything about kissing Alexei felt right, though it should not.

It most definitely should *not.*

But she was caught in the grip of new feelings, of the excitement and danger of kissing this dark, hard man.

Paige threaded a gloved hand into the hair at his nape, let the other slip beneath his coat to wander over the hard muscles of his chest. He made a sound of approval. And then his lips left hers, trailed hot kisses along her jaw to her ear.

"Alexei," she breathed, his name turning to frost as he sought her lips again. Whatever she'd been about to say was lost as he kissed her into a quivering bundle of nerve endings and sexual excitement.

"You are so beautiful. I want you, Paige," he said. "Now. Tonight."

Their mouths fused once more, and her spirit soared. Whatever the past, whatever the future—*this* moment was right. She couldn't have him forever, but she could have him right now. And why not? She deserved her own slice of happiness, for however long it lasted.

A little voice inside her head tried to interject reason, but she refused to listen. She'd been listening to that little voice for the last eight years, and it hadn't gotten her anything but loneliness and heartache.

"Yes," she said between kisses. "Yes."

The ride back to the palace took no time at all. Alexei turned the horses and gave them rein until the *troika* was whisking across the snow at a smart pace. Behind them the wolves howled, but in the sled, Paige felt safe and warm. Soon they were gliding into the courtyard, and then Alexei was handing the reins to a groom and lifting her from the sleigh.

They raced into the house like a couple of children, Alexei holding her hand and tugging her up the grand staircase. She felt like a princess in her white coat and fur hat, and she laughed when Alexei threw open a door and pulled her inside. Then he was slamming the door, his fingers flying over the buttons of her coat as he walked her backward.

"I have wanted to get you out of this uptight suit since I first saw you this morning," he said, his voice hot and sexy as he slipped the coat from her shoulders and tossed it aside. The hat and scarf followed, and she tugged off her gloves so she could feel his skin beneath her fingertips.

This morning. Was it really only this morning that they'd faced each other in a boardroom? Paige extinguished the thought before she could dwell on it. She knew who she was with, and she knew why it was wrong.

But she didn't want to stop. She wanted to race recklessly forward, before sense caught up with her. She wanted to feel *alive* for one night, wanted to feel the passion and power of a man moving inside her.

This man.

It was only once, only tonight. Tomorrow, she would go back to being staid Paige Barnes, efficient secretary.

Alexei got out of his coat before she could do it for him, and then he started to work on the buttons of her blouse. Paige slipped his shirt from his waistband and ran her hands beneath, finally touching his hot skin.

He flinched, laughing. "Your hands are cold."

"So are yours," she said when he slipped a finger beneath the edge of her bra. But she was too hot to care. His touch soothed the sizzle, gave her hope he would quench this fire before the evening was through.

Crazy, crazy, crazy.

She could hear the chant in her head, but she didn't want to listen to it. There would be plenty of time for self-recrimination later. Now, she only wanted to feel how good it could be with him.

Alexei's mouth sought hers as he slid the blouse from her shoulders. Paige met him eagerly, arching into his touch like a cat. *Don't think; just feel.*

He broke away and ripped his shirt over his head, then kissed her again, his hands sliding to the waistband of her trousers. A cold shot of fear darted through her, threatening to douse her ardor.

Should she explain that she was inexperienced? That she'd only done this once before, and she wasn't even sure if it counted?

But if she did, would he stop? She couldn't stand the idea that her inexperience might make the difference in whether or not he found her desirable, so she didn't say anything.

Another moment, and her pants were gone, sliding down her legs to pool at her feet before she stepped out of them.

The heat in Alexei's eyes was so intense she felt scorched from the contact. He spoke in Russian, exotic words she had no hope of understanding. She started to fold her arms beneath her breasts, but he stopped her.

"I would have never guessed that you had naughty undergarments beneath that suit."

Paige blushed. "They aren't naughty. They're just lacy."

And maybe a little bit racy. Her bra was white lace, fairly staid, but she'd worn a thong beneath her pants because it left no panty line.

Alexei made a spinning motion with his finger. She turned in an awkward circle before facing him again.

"You are very beautiful, Paige."

Part of her wanted to tell him to stop saying it, that she wasn't beautiful at all, but another part wanted to believe every word.

"You have too many clothes on," she said, unable to bear

his scrutiny a moment more while he was still partially clothed.

"Then help me to lose them."

She reached for his belt buckle, slipped it open. His bare chest radiated so much heat she thought she would burn. Last night, she'd seen the shadows of muscle and sinew beneath his open shirt, but that hadn't prepared her for the sight of him. He was broad-shouldered, beautifully made, with tight muscle and silky skin. Heart in her throat, Paige tugged his zipper down.

He took over, shedding his trousers until he stood before her completely naked. Paige swallowed a bubble of apprehension. He was magnificent, tall and broad, with clearly defined stomach muscles, and a dark, sexy arrow of hair pointing a trail down his abdomen.

"Do you like what you see?" he murmured, and Paige's gaze snapped to his. She'd been staring at his penis, hadn't she? But he was hard, ready for her—and clearly unembarrassed by his state of arousal.

Oh, God.

Paige felt as if she were stuck to the floor. She didn't know how she was supposed to act now. What would a sophisticated woman do? Would she go to him, wrap her arms around him and purr in his ear? Or would she shed her underwear and drape herself artfully across the bed?

Thankfully Alexei had no such problem deciding what to do. Sweeping her up, he carried her to the bed and laid her down. She could hardly process the luxury of her surroundings—the bed was canopied, gilded, and draped with thick, rich velvet. Inside the canopy dome, someone had painted a scene of a man and woman in a *troika,* the horses stretched out as they flew across a snowy landscape.

"You are trembling," he said as he came down beside her on the crisp cotton sheets. "Do I frighten you?"

"No, but it's been a long time," she admitted.

It was true, in a way. It *had* been a long time since she'd lost her virginity to a guy from her accounting class. Bob, who drank too much, botched the job and never called again. She'd always imagined it was out of embarrassment rather than because of anything she'd done.

Now she was beginning to worry that she might have been wrong.

"Then we will take our time," Alexei said, removing her glasses and placing them on the nightstand. "I can imagine nothing more pleasurable."

His mouth came down on hers, and her body melted by degrees. When Alexei kissed her, she felt that she would do anything he asked. It must be true, considering that she was naked in his bed and more than four hundred miles away from where she was supposed to be.

Except that he hadn't kissed her at all tonight until they'd gone on the *troika* ride. Everything that she'd done up to that point was her own doing, not a result of coercion.

Nor was this, she admitted to herself.

Alexei reached beneath her, found the catch to her bra and unsnapped it. Then he tugged it off and tossed it aside before cupping her breasts in his hands and kissing first one nipple and then the other while she squirmed beneath him.

"You are most sensitive," he murmured against her flesh. "I like you this way."

When his lips closed over her nipple, sweetly sucking it into a hard point, Paige gasped and arched her back. He obliged her by sucking harder.

"You like this," he said. Goose bumps rose on her flesh where his hot tongue left a wet trail to her other breast. Then he was repeating the motions again and again, sucking each of her nipples until she thought she would scream from the pure pleasure of it.

"Alexei," she gasped. "I don't want to go slow anymore!"

She was burning up, aching for him in ways she'd never experienced.

He chuckled. "Patience, sweet one. We have plenty of time." He kissed her stomach, rolled his tongue around her belly button and then traced a line across the top of her thong. "This is very sexy underwear, Paige Barnes. You make me wonder what other surprises you have in store."

And then he pushed her panties down her hips until she had no barriers left. Her breath caught in her throat.

She thought she was prepared for what he did next, but how could you be prepared for a thing you'd never experienced?

Alexei pushed her legs open, teased her with hot kisses along the insides of her thighs—but when he spread her wide and touched her with his tongue, Paige couldn't suppress the little scream that escaped. She thought she would literally fly apart.

Her entire body was on fire. Her hair tingled. And Alexei's mouth did things to her that no man had ever done. She wanted it to last forever—

But it was over in a matter of seconds as her body reached an impossibly high peak, and then dove into a free fall. Paige cried out, gasping and sobbing for breath during the long journey to the bottom.

The experience was intense, amazing, far more than she'd ever dreamed.

Yet still it wasn't over.

She thought Alexei would enter her body now, but he brought her to the peak once more with his mouth, and, when she thought she couldn't possibly take any more, he did it a third time.

She was wrung-out, sated, her body quivering with pleasure—and still she craved more.

"Please, Alexei," she said as he moved away from her. "Don't go."

His laugh was deep, sexy. "I'm not leaving, Paige. Not for a long time."

He reached into the table beside the bed, and then he was rolling on a condom and settling himself over top of her. She wrapped her legs around him, knowing instinctively that this was what she was supposed to do. He kissed her sweetly while he entered her body, moving forward on a long, slow glide that made her moan.

The pleasure took her breath away, even while the size and feel of him was almost too much. There was a moment of pain, a sharp sensation of tearing—and then he was inside her fully, his body throbbing in the very core of her.

"You should have told me," he gasped out.

When she opened her eyes, the expression on his face tore her heart in two. He looked lost, alone—confused, as if he'd expected one thing and gotten another.

Paige's heart dropped. "Told you what? Have I done something wrong?"

"You're a virgin." He seemed angry, intense.

Shock momentarily stole her voice. "I can't be."

He groaned as she moved beneath him. "Trust me, you are. *Were*."

"I've been with one man. He, um…" She could feel her face turning red as she struggled to say it. "He barely started before he was finished."

Meaning he'd started to enter her body, and then stiffened as his climax hit him. Her first sexual experience had been over before it ever really began. Which meant he'd not taken her virginity as she'd always thought. He'd only started the job. Alexei had just now completed it.

Alexei's expression changed, grew fierce suddenly. But it wasn't the kind of fierce that scared her. Or at least not in a bad way. No, it was an intense, possessive, determined kind of look that said he wasn't about to quit until they were completely, thoroughly finished.

"My God, Paige," he said. "Just when I think you cannot surprise me any more than you already have."

His mouth came down on hers, hot, possessive. She relaxed into his kiss for only a moment before he set her body on fire with his own. He was gloriously hard, moving, his body showing no signs of being done.

Her heart soared. This was really happening, they were really making love—it wasn't going to end with him apologizing, grabbing his clothes, leaving her alone and wondering what the hell had just happened.

She couldn't think of anything but him as the wave caught her and tossed her higher than she'd ever been.

She learned very quickly how to shift her hips up to meet him, how to open herself to him, and how to prolong her pleasure and stave off the inevitable—but only for so long, because Alexei was relentless, driving her toward a completion more intense than any she'd experienced before now.

When her orgasm hit her this time, she couldn't hold back the scream that had pooled at the base of her throat. Vaguely she was aware that he followed her over the edge. Moments later he rolled over, taking her with him until she was lying on top of him, his body still buried deep inside hers.

Instinctively she knew that nothing would ever be the same again.

CHAPTER SEVEN

NOTHING HAD GONE the way he'd expected. Alexei lay beneath her, wondering what in the hell had just happened to him. Everything had spiraled out of control the instant he'd kissed her in the sleigh. He had not meant to move so fast.

He'd intended a slower seduction, perhaps unfolding over the next few days. And he'd intended to get inside her head, to have her open up to him and trust him before they went to bed.

He'd intended, bastard that he was, to make her think he was falling for her. Paige Barnes was the kind of woman who should be eating out of his hand.

And yet she was not. Nor did she seem likely to.

Which, paradoxically, might explain this intense attraction he felt toward her. She was so much more than he'd expected, and every moment he spent with her only increased his fascination.

My God, she'd still been a virgin. He hadn't counted on that at all. Guilt stabbed him in the gut. She'd trusted him enough to give him her virginity, and all he'd intended was to take advantage of her.

But how could he have known? He'd entered her so easily that he'd barely noticed the slight resistance until he'd broken through it. Then he'd been blown away.

She'd turned the tables on him with her sweet innocence

and earthy sexuality. The contrast between the two fascinated him. Compelled him. Even before he'd known she was still a virgin, he'd wanted her like he couldn't remember ever wanting another woman in recent memory.

Or ever?

Alexei closed his eyes. No, of course not. He must have wanted another woman this badly. What about Fermina, the supermodel? She'd had the longest legs he'd ever seen.

But, no. She'd been delightful, not compelling.

He ran through a succession of women in his head. None conjured up more than pleasant memories. None conjured up violent need that spiraled out of his control.

Perhaps it was the excitement of making love to Chad Russell's secretary, of taking something from under his cousin's nose that the man had been too ignorant to see for himself.

But, no, it wasn't that, either.

Paige's warm body was limp, her breathing even, and he knew she'd fallen asleep. He wanted to sleep as well, but he could not. He was still inside her, still hard, but he needed to withdraw while the condom was still tight.

Except that he didn't want to move. He wanted to lie here, sated and content, and enjoy the warm woman in his bed. He wanted to enjoy the companionship with her, however brief.

Paige knew what it was like to lose family too soon. It was a connection they shared. Another reason everything about this night seemed so strange to him. He didn't usually share details about his family with the women he dated.

Hell, he didn't usually share details of his life and family with *anyone*. He'd learned that life wasn't fair, and that you couldn't trust another soul with the burdens of yours. No one was what he or she seemed. Everyone had an agenda of some sort.

And his was to destroy the Russells.

Not that he'd told her much, but he'd said more than he usually did. In the instant when he'd told her that his family was in the crypt, he'd felt a wall of loneliness pushing down on him that he hadn't experienced in a very long time. Somehow, she'd recognized it. He'd wanted to open up to her even more in that moment, but he'd stopped himself from doing so.

She did something to him, something he did not like. She made him long for things he'd forgotten, and feel remorse for things he could not help if he were to avenge his family. He had no room for sentimentality, no room for tender feelings of any kind.

A glance at the bedside clock told him it was nearly ten. A few more minutes, and he would wake her—though part of him wanted to keep her in his bed all night, to slide into her body in the dark hours before dawn, to lose himself.

But he would not. The sooner he returned her to Moscow, the better.

The sharp, insistent ringing of a cell phone startled Paige into wakefulness. Beside her, Alexei whipped back the covers and shot from the bed. His phone was still clipped onto his trousers, but he managed to grab it before it stopped ringing.

"Da?" he barked.

Paige sat up, her body protesting the movement. Though she wanted to stay snuggled into bed, where it was warm, it was time to return to reality.

Reality for her was not a naked billionaire pacing the room and barking into his phone in a language she didn't understand.

She took the opportunity, while he wasn't paying attention, to slip from the bed and start collecting her clothes. It took a few moments to locate her underwear, but when she had everything she darted into the attached bathroom.

Paige leaned back against the closed door, blinking in

disbelief. Yet another beautiful, fairy-tale room. Though at least there were modern fixtures—a shower, toilet and claw-foot bathtub with jets. Clearly Alexei had upgraded a few things.

She wondered why he and his mother and sister had been sent away from this place, but she'd hardly been able to ask. What must it have been like to be so young and to not only lose your father, but to also find yourself thrown out of your home? How had his poor mother handled everything with two young children to look after?

Paige felt a pang of emotion for the woman lying in the church crypt. And for the man who seemed so in control and detached when he spoke of his family, yet who was so alive and full of fire. A fire that had nearly incinerated them both when he'd focused it on her.

She set her clothes on a tufted bench and turned on the water in the sink so she could wash her face.

And did a double take at the woman staring at her in the mirror. My God, was that her?

Her hair was mussed, of course, but it was her face that shocked her. Her lips were red, swollen from kissing, and her eyes were lazy, sensual. Her mascara had smeared, but instead of looking like a Gothic vampire, it made her look tousled. Like she was a sex goddess who'd been making love all night long.

She took a step back, let her gaze wander down her body. Her skin glowed. She looked happy. Pretty. Was that what sexual satisfaction did to a person?

If so, she'd certainly missed out on a lot. She could barely process that she'd technically still been a virgin. She was slightly sore, but not so much so that her body didn't leap at the idea of doing it all again.

A sharp rap sounded on the door and she jumped. "Yes?"

"We must go, Paige," Alexei said. "The helicopter is waiting."

His voice was impersonal, sharp, and her stomach dropped. Whatever she'd expected after tonight, the indifference in his voice hadn't been it. Hadn't they just shared something beautiful? And, more than their bodies, hadn't they shared a bit of their souls with each other?

It had certainly felt like it, especially when he'd insisted on pointing out to her that she'd been living for Emma and it was time to stop. Or when he'd told her with such stark pain in his gaze that his family was buried in the crypt.

"I'm coming," she said, stiffening her resolve. She would not let him know how far out of her depth she was, how much this night meant to her. He was already behaving as if it was over, so she would do the same. Time to return to their proper roles as wary strangers.

She could do that. She *would* do that.

Paige hurriedly washed her face and got dressed. She hadn't been able to find the elastic that she'd held her ponytail back with, so she did the best she could with her unruly hair before opening the door.

Alexei stood in the middle of the room, talking on his phone once more. He was fully dressed—in different clothes, naturally, which made her feel rather cheap and, well, transitory. He did not look up when she walked into the room, and her heart squeezed into a painful knot.

What had she expected? She'd known what she was getting into when she'd said yes.

He finally glanced over at her, something flashing across his face before he looked away again. She picked up her coat and stood waiting. He motioned her to the door, opening it for her, then following once she'd gone through. She stepped back to let him take the lead. He didn't look at her while he walked down the hallway and descended the stairs.

Paige's skin was hot, but for a different reason than when they'd burst up these steps earlier. Then, she'd been giddy with excitement. Now, she felt like a prostitute he'd picked up on the street. He'd brought her home for a quick screw and now he was done with her.

She lifted her chin, determined not to let him see how much his indifference hurt and confused her. She hadn't expected a declaration of true love, but she'd thought they would at least act like two people who'd shared something intimate together.

They stopped at the door they'd entered earlier. Alexei put his phone away and donned the coat he'd been carrying. Paige did the same, settling the hat into place and wrapping the scarf around her neck. Stuffing her hands into her pockets, she realized she'd forgotten the gloves. But she wasn't going back for them.

There was no time anyway.

The man who'd greeted them earlier stood by the ornately carved door. He and Alexei spoke briefly, and then he was opening the door as Alexei turned and took her by the elbow.

"Watch your step," Alexei said as they emerged into the frigid night air.

"Spokojnoj Nochi," the man called out before shutting the huge door behind them.

The *whop-whop-whop* of the helicopter rotors sounded nearby, as well as a scratching sound that she realized was the top layer of snow being disturbed in the vortex.

When they were safely onboard, the craft lifted into the air and banked to the right. Paige stared down at the ghostly shadow of the Voronov Palace, huge and hulking on the pristine snow. She half expected the ground to open up and swallow it whole, like a sacred location that disappeared after you'd completed a quest.

SAVE OVER £39 25% OFF

Sign up to get 4 stories a month for 12 months in advance and **SAVE £39.60 – that's a fantastic 25% off**
If you prefer you can sign up for 6 months in advance and **SAVE £15.84 – that's still an impressive 20% off**

FULL PRICE	PER-PAID SUBSCRIPTION PRICE	SAVINGS	MONTHS
£158.40	£118.80	25%	12
£79.20	£63.36	20%	6

- **FREE P&P** Your books will be delivered direct to your door every month for FREE

- **Plus** to say thank you, we will send you a **FREE** L'Occitane gift set worth over **£10**

  Gift set has a RRP of £10.50 and includes Verbena Shower Gel 75m and Soap 110g

What's more you will receive ALL of these additional benefits

- Be the FIRST to receive the most up-to-date titles
- FREE P&P
- Lots of free gifts and exciting special offers
- Monthly exclusive newsletter
- Special REWARDS programme
- No Obligation –
  You can cancel your subscription at any time
  by writing to us at Mills & Boon Book Club,
  PO Box 676, Richmond, TW9 1WU.

MILLS & BOON

Sign up to save online at www.millsandboon.co.uk

P1AIT

Twenty minutes later, they were boarding Alexei's private jet. Alexei hadn't spoken a word to her since he'd told her to watch her step. Instead he'd been on the phone, on his computer, his concentration intense and undivided. A flight attendant came over and asked if she would like something to drink.

"No, thank you," she replied. After the woman left, Paige tried to close her eyes and rest. It was nearly eleven-thirty, and though she had no idea what Chad's plans were for tomorrow, she had to get up and be ready in case he needed her to do something.

Hot guilt sizzled through her like a brand. She'd been reckless, and now she was regretting the impulse. The man she'd risked her job for had been ignoring her almost since the moment he'd found his release in her body.

It stung her pride, and yet she'd gone into it with eyes wide-open. She had no one to blame but herself.

She was aware of the moment he snapped his computer closed. Aware of the dark, powerful energy radiating from him as his voice went silent. Presumably he was finished with his call.

He said something that sounded like an order. When the flight attendant answered, Paige knew she'd guessed right.

A minute later something popped. It almost sounded like a gun. Paige sat up ramrod straight, her eyes darting to Alexei. He held a glass of champagne, his smile devilish as he lifted it in her direction.

"Madam," a soft voice said, and Paige realized the flight attendant was holding out a glass for her. She took it before looking to Alexei again.

His face had been transformed once more, and her heart thumped against her chest. He was so handsome, so sexy. And so lonely, she thought.

No. She would not feel empathy for him, not now.

"What are we drinking to?" she said as coolly as she could manage. Two could play this game.

"Triumph," he replied before taking a long swallow.

Paige's blood froze in her veins. She set the glass down. "What are you saying?"

But she knew. Oh, God, she knew.

"Chad Russell is broke, is he not? This was his last chance to salvage his company." He took another sip of champagne while her heart refused to beat. "His financiers have pulled out of the deal."

Chad would be destroyed. And Emma's happiness along with him. Paige was halfway out of her seat—to do what she didn't know—before Alexei's cruel laugh stopped her.

"Ah yes, you did know something, though you claimed you did not. I can see it written on your face."

Hatred broke the ice in her veins, pumped hot blood into her heart. She'd known the deal was life or death to Chad, but she hadn't known the extent of it. "Then I guess we both lied. This was all a game, wasn't it? You only pretended to want me."

He stretched like a cat before rising from his seat and coming over to plop down into the plush club chair next to hers. "Ah, no," he said, his gray gaze slipping over her, "I did not pretend. I think that should be clear based on what we shared tonight."

Outrage and self-loathing were a vile stew inside her. How had she fallen for this? How? "You brought me here to seduce me. You arranged the nice dinner, the *troika*—"

She broke off, unable to continue. She'd let herself go, let herself enjoy and believe—for a short time—that a prince could be interested in a dull secretary.

What a joke.

"*Da,* I arranged it all," he said matter-of-factly. "But that does not mean I didn't enjoy it."

She turned away from him. Evil man. Worst of all, she'd actually felt something with him. The wonder and beauty of what he'd done to her, the intensity of her response—it was more than she'd ever experienced before.

And now the memory was ruined.

"Come, Paige, do not act so hurt. This was war. You and I both knew it."

She collected her emotions, turned back to him. "Don't drag me down to your level. I'm nothing like you. I don't use people."

"Are you not? I seem to remember that you were the one who wanted me to make love to you last night in my apartment." He tipped a finger under her chin when she would have turned away again, held her steady while his hot eyes bored into her. "You wanted to use me to forget what Chad had done to you."

Her conscience burned with the truth of what he was saying. And yet it wasn't the same at all. "I told you that Chad and I weren't involved. He didn't do *anything* to me."

"But you wanted him to," Alexei said. "You wanted *him* to be the man who made love to you."

"No," she breathed—and yet he'd stated the truth. She'd thought she'd wanted her boss as her lover, thought he was the perfect man. But she knew, after tonight, that she couldn't have done with Chad what she'd done with Alexei.

"Deny it all you like," he said. "But we both know the truth."

"Why do you hate him so much?" she asked.

A shadow crossed his features. "Who said anything about hate? This is business."

Paige shook her head. "No, it's more than that. I saw the way you looked at him today."

"Perhaps you should ask him," Alexei said, his jaw tightening. She got the impression he'd said more than he intended with that short sentence.

"I can't do that and you know it."

He set the empty champagne glass down on the table in front of them and stood. "You can do anything you wish, *maya krasavitsa*. As of tomorrow, you will no longer be working for Chad Russell."

"I won't work for you, either," she blurted.

He scoffed. "Don't be stupid, Paige. You need the money."

Though fear made her pulse throb in her temples, she knew she couldn't work for Alexei Voronov. It was the one thing she could do for herself, the one way to reclaim her self-respect. After a night of self-indulgent folly, she could stand firm on this one thing.

"I'd rather clean toilets for a living before working for a man I hate."

He bent over her chair, cupping his hands on either side of her face before she could stop him. His mouth claimed hers in a hard, dominant kiss. Fury whipped through her with tornado strength and she clamped her lips tight against his. He answered her by gripping her jaw hard enough to force her mouth open.

And then he was inside, kissing her with the heat and strength of earlier. When she bit down on his tongue, he laughed and clamped his fingers around her jaw again until she released him.

The kiss turned explosive, with him bending her back in the seat and her taking as much as he could give. Never again would she be meek or easily manipulated.

This was an angry kiss, a kiss of war, but a hot kiss nonetheless. When he broke away, she whimpered in response before she could stop herself.

But she wasn't the only one affected. His eyes were wild

as he gazed down at her, hot and dark and full of need. He thrust a hand through his dark hair, pulled in a deep breath.

And then he was collected once more, staring down at her with such coolness that she shivered. "Oh, yes, Paige Barnes," he threw at her, "you definitely hate me. If we had more time, I would show you exactly how much."

CHAPTER EIGHT

One month later...

PAIGE HIT THE alarm, flopping back into bed with a groggy sigh. Six o'clock seemed to come earlier and earlier each morning. For the past two weeks, she'd had such trouble waking up. It wasn't jet lag; they'd returned to Dallas a month ago, and she'd been over the jet lag within a few days.

But she'd gotten more and more tired with each passing day, as if she needed a shot of caffeine straight to her veins to get her moving. She drank coffee every morning, but by noon she was dragging again. By the time she got home, she was ready for bed.

Nothing had been right since she'd left Russia. She'd started a new job at a downtown law firm just last week, thanks to Mavis, who'd recently taken a job there because she'd also refused to work for Alexei after spending so many years with Chad and his father. The pay, at least for Paige, wasn't as good as it had been at Russell Tech, but she'd gone over her budget and figured out how to pay all her bills and stay in the same house she'd been renting for the past three years.

It was tight, but it worked.

Somehow, Paige managed to haul herself from the bed and throw on her robe. Before she could hit the shower, she needed a cup of coffee.

"You look like hell," Emma said when she entered the kitchen.

"Thanks," Paige replied as she grabbed a mug and filled it.

She didn't bother to tell Emma that she looked like hell, too. For a different reason, of course. Since they'd returned to Texas, she'd barely seen Chad. He was off in Alaska, trying to drum up business with some of his father's old acquaintances. He'd poured his personal fortune into Russell Tech over the last few years. When the company went broke, he had, too.

There was no question of a wedding anytime soon. Paige secretly added *if ever,* though it hurt her to do so. Emma tried to be brave, but Paige heard her crying at night sometimes. She hated Alexei Voronov for many things, but for that most of all.

Paige took a sip of coffee, waiting for the pleasurable little jolt. But the flavor turned her stomach instead. She set the cup back down, frowning. "What are you doing up so early?"

Emma's brows drew together as she studied Paige. "I have final exams today. Are you sick?"

Paige put her hands to either side of her head. She'd asked herself that question every day. "I don't know."

"You look pale. Maybe you should stay home."

"I can't. I'm too new and I don't have any sick leave yet."

"But you're not well. I'm sure they'll work something out. If you want, I'll call Mavis for you."

Paige waved a hand. "No, don't do that. I'll be fine as soon as I shower."

But when she stood beneath the hot spray, she didn't feel better at all; she felt ill. Her stomach heaved, and before she could get to the toilet, she was sick. Since there was nothing in her stomach, it was over quickly.

Maybe Emma was right. Maybe she'd caught something

at work, though no one seemed to be sick at Fennell, Brown, and Ramirez.

Paige finished her shower, dragged on a pair of dark slacks and a powder-blue top and headed for work without attempting to eat breakfast since food was impossible.

The morning passed torturously. Paige tried to eat one of the doughnuts Mavis had brought in, but the first bite shot bile up into her throat. She ran to the toilet three times and threw up twice, though she'd eaten nothing at all.

The third time she returned to her desk, Mavis was frowning at her.

"You look like death warmed over, sugar," the older woman said. "Are you feeling okay?"

Paige settled into her chair very carefully. The document she'd been working on was still open on her computer, the cursor blinking at her accusingly.

"I think I must have eaten something bad," she said, taking a sip of her bottled water.

Mavis shoved a pencil in her steel-gray hair. Mavis's hair was a good five inches tall, having been teased and sprayed to within an inch of its life. Paige had often wondered if Mavis got home at the end of the day and discovered bits of flotsam she'd shoved in there during work. Stray pencils, an eraser, correction tape.

Mavis's face scrunched in concentration. "Could be, but seems like you'd be a lot sicker a whole lot quicker, if you know what I mean." She tilted her head to the side. "This has been going on for a while. Can you keep anything down?"

"Not this morning."

"Any other symptoms?"

"I've been tired a lot, but I think it must be leftover jet lag or something. I can hardly get out of bed in the morning."

The corners of Mavis's eyes crinkled as she screwed her

face up even tighter. "Now, darlin', you don't have a boyfriend or anything do you?"

Paige shook her head. "You know I don't."

"I thought so, sweetie, but things could have changed."

"Why do you ask?"

"Well, if you did, I'd be wanting to know when you'd last had your period. Because if it'd been a while, you might want to pee on a stick."

"Pee on a stick?" *Oh, dear God.*

Mavis mistook her statement for an actual question. "Honey, I'm talking about a pregnancy test," she said in her syrupy accent, drawing the word *test* into two syllables. "But since it can't be that, maybe you should go to the doctor and see if you got that swine flu or something. Though you sure do remind me of my daughter when she was pregnant with the twins. Poor girl couldn't keep a thing down for weeks. Slept all the time, too."

A frisson of icy fear danced down Paige's spine. It wasn't possible. Alexei had used a condom, and they'd only had sex once. There was no way she was pregnant!

But her brain was working overtime, doing the math, and she realized it'd been a while since her last period. She just didn't know how long. For that, she'd have to dig into her purse and check her pocket calendar. She always noted the date since it seemed to be the first thing the doctor's office wanted to know each time she went in for an appointment. Didn't matter what the appointment was for, they always wanted to know the answer.

The phone rang and Mavis answered it, sparing Paige from continuing the conversation. She opened a desk drawer and quickly located her calendar in the bottom of her purse. Flipping back, she found the date and counted forward.

Six weeks.

But that didn't mean anything. Stress could delay ovulation, which meant her period could start any day really. Paige closed her eyes and took a deep breath. Surely that's all it was. Stress, and a stomach bug.

But she knew she would worry until her period showed up. More worry meant more stress. More stress meant more delay, which meant no period.

The only way to ease her mind was to stop at the drugstore on the way home tonight.

Unbelievable.

She put the calendar away with shaky hands and tried to concentrate on the document. Half an hour later, kindly Mr. Ramirez emerged from his office and ordered her to go home.

She wanted to argue, but the truth was she just wanted to go curl up on the couch with the remote. When Mr. Ramirez assured her she would be paid for the hours she would miss, Paige logged off her computer and gathered her things.

By the time she got home, she felt better. But the package in her hand had the power to change everything.

She slipped the pregnancy test out of the bag and stared at it. Her heart hammered. Was this really necessary? Was it possible?

Anything was possible, she supposed. Practically, she was just ruling out a possibility, however remote, so she could focus on what might actually be wrong. When the test came out negative, she would call her doctor and schedule an appointment. Maybe she was allergic to something, or maybe she'd picked up a strange virus in Russia.

Twenty minutes later, after she read the instructions twice, Paige peed in a cup and inserted the stick—she didn't want any mistakes—and then removed it after the appropriate amount of time. While the stick did its magic, she crossed to the kitchen and peered inside the fridge. Her stomach was growling now, and she felt like she could eat something without getting sick.

Grabbing a yogurt, she popped the top and dipped her spoon inside before returning to where she'd laid the stick on the bathroom counter. It hadn't been more than a minute, but the digital window had an answer.

The spoon clattered into the sink as her fingers lost the ability to hold it.

Pregnant.

Paige snatched up the test and held it closer. Maybe there was a glare on her glasses that was obscuring the *not*. But the window was very clear.

Oh, God, she was pregnant! With a Russian prince's baby. It didn't seem real, didn't seem possible.

Yet the test did not lie. Paige made it to the couch before she sank into a boneless heap. What now?

She pressed her hand to her abdomen. Was there really a little life in there? A baby who was half her and half Alexei?

Her mind threw out possibilities in dizzying succession. She could terminate the pregnancy and no one would ever know. She could carry the baby to term and give it up for adoption. Or she could keep her baby.

Her fingers clenched reflexively. Already, she felt protective. And she knew what she was going to do. She *wanted* this baby with a fierceness that surprised her. She would keep her child, and she would raise him or her alone. It would be tough, especially now, but she knew what tough was. She already had experience with working herself to the bone to provide for a child.

So this would be a new experience, starting from the earliest moments of life, but she would adapt.

What about Alexei?

Paige chewed her lip. Should she try to get in contact

with him? Tell him about his child? Her mind rebelled at the thought. He was a cold, cruel man who'd pretended to be something he was not.

He'd pretended to be kind and solicitous, and he'd pretended an interest in her for the sole purpose of using her for information. When he no longer needed that information, he'd discarded her like yesterday's garbage. And he'd made no effort to get in contact since. He'd managed to find Emma when she was in Chad's hotel room, so Paige had no illusions about his ability to find her in Dallas if he so chose. He just didn't want to find her.

In fact, though it hurt to know, he probably gave her no thought whatsoever. Since the second he'd dropped her off at her hotel, he'd erased her from his mind.

She knew because she'd seen a photo of him at a Hollywood movie premiere recently. He'd been escorting a gorgeous starlet who'd clung to his arm and smiled at him as if he were the center of the universe.

Paige had quickly shoved aside the pang of jealousy she'd felt. The starlet would find out soon enough how cruel Alexei could be. He might seem like a prize to be coveted, but he certainly was not.

She thought of her sister, and her hatred for Alexei simmered.

No, she would not try to contact him. He'd made it clear what his feelings about their night together had been. It was one night that he'd already forgotten, and she was the one who would have to deal with the consequences.

Alexei told himself that he simply wanted to return the gloves she'd left behind. And the coat, scarf and hat that she'd posted to him before she left Russia. He'd been angry when he'd opened the box and realized what was inside.

Yet he should have expected it. Paige was proud and

stubborn and it would be just like her to try to have the last word.

He'd wondered why she'd only kept the gloves, but it wasn't until he'd returned to St. Petersburg the following weekend that he'd found them lying neatly on the nightstand and realized what had happened. A maid must have put them there, because he remembered quite vividly how Paige had stripped them off and thrown them aside so she could touch him.

Alexei closed his eyes. *So she could touch him.*

He could remember, even now, the sizzle of her skin against his, the heat and passion that had threatened to incinerate him. He remembered wanting to be inside her with an urgency that had surprised him with its intensity.

He hadn't been with a woman since that night. He'd thought about it. He'd even gone out with a beautiful actress recently, but the night ended when he took her back to her apartment and left her at the door with a chaste kiss.

She simply hadn't excited him.

Paige had. Paige Barnes, who wore dull suits and glasses and who'd kissed him like she needed his touch in order to survive.

He'd wanted to see her again, but he'd resisted the impulse. Now that he was in Dallas to explore his latest acquisition, he didn't have to wait. He would see her and he would return the damn coat he'd bought her.

Russell Tech was finally his, and though he'd thought he would take great pleasure in entering those hallowed offices as the owner rather than as a supplicant begging for his sister's life, it hadn't been as sweet as he'd thought it would be. For a moment, as he'd stood in that office where Tim Russell had refused to help him and gazed out on the Dallas skyline, he'd felt emptier inside than he ever had before.

Why?

The limo he'd hired drove him from his hotel through the

outskirts of Dallas and into a suburban neighborhood with small bungalows and green lawns. Paige had kept her word and left Russell Tech, but he knew she worked at a law firm and he knew she would be home by now. He'd thought about going to her office, but decided it was better they see each other in private.

What would she say when she saw him again? Would he see a flash of that sweet desire she'd never quite been able to hide? Or would she now look at him with abject hatred? He wanted the former and hoped, for her sake, it was the latter.

Because, though he shouldn't still want her, he did. As much as he would find the experience of bedding her pleasurable, he had nothing else to give her. He'd already taken enough from her. He would not take more, even if he couldn't quite stop himself from delivering the coat in person.

Finally the car pulled to a halt in front of a brown house with a covered porch. It was a cute home. Cozy. The grass was manicured, but not too much so. The flower beds weren't overflowing with plants, though they were neat and clean. It was as if someone cared about the garden, but didn't have a lot of time to fuss over it.

Alexei grabbed the garment bag he'd brought and strode to the door. He rang the bell and waited. A gray-haired woman in a pink housedress stood on the front porch next door, staring at him. He gave her a smile, which only seemed to fluster her. She hurried inside, but he didn't miss the curtain inching back on the window facing Paige's house.

Finally the mint-green door swung open. He wasn't sure what he'd expected to happen when he saw her again, but the immediate rush of blood to his groin was certainly not it.

"Hello, Paige," he said softly, his gaze slipping down her body. She was dressed in a pair of shorts that showed her lovely long legs, and a tank top that clung to her generous breasts. Her dark hair was pulled back in the usual ponytail.

But her face did not look happy at all. Her eyes shot daggers at him and her lips were pinched at the corners. "Nice to see you, too."

"What are you doing here?" she demanded.

He held up the garment bag. "Returning your coat."

Her fingers were bloodless where they clamped the door. "I don't want it, Prince Voronov. Thank you for coming by, but please leave."

"Ah, so we are back to that now. How formal and polite you are, Paige, considering what we've done to each other."

He loved the blush staining her cheeks. So innocent, and so sensual all at once. That's what he remembered, what he craved.

"I—" She turned green. If he hadn't been looking at her, he wouldn't have believed it. "Excuse me," she said, turning and bolting into the house.

Alexei walked into the entry and closed the door behind him. He tossed the garment bag on a chair and followed the sounds of retching to the small bath in the hall.

"Paige? What is wrong? Do you need a doctor?"

"No," she said miserably, her voice loud and clear through the closed door. "I'll feel better when you leave. So get out. And take the coat with you!"

"As you wish," he said, though he had no intention of doing so. Instead he retreated to the tiny kitchen nearby and sat on a bar stool to wait. The kitchen opened into a small living room furnished with an oversize couch, a couple of chairs, and a television. It wasn't sumptuous by any stretch, and yet he found himself drawn to the homey feel.

After his father had died, he'd lived in a house not much bigger than this. His mother had tried to make it homey, but they didn't have much to live on. All she'd gotten when his father died was a small sum of money and some land everyone had thought was worthless. He'd loved their land as a child.

They might not have had much money, but he and Katerina had played for hours in the woods and creeks. They'd fished, hunted and climbed the trees like monkeys.

They'd been happy, in spite of their lack. Kids didn't care, so long as they were loved and had enough food to eat.

More than anything, he'd wanted to give his mother back the lifestyle she'd had when she'd been a princess in a fairy-tale palace. He'd worked tirelessly, but his true success came too late.

Now that he had his family palace back, and homes in several countries, none of them gave him that feeling of comfort he wanted, that feeling he remembered from his childhood. This house had that feeling. Two minutes inside its interior and he knew the feeling was here.

Home. It was more than simply furniture or belongings. It was an indefinable *feeling*. His heart longed for it, and yet it was something he'd been denied for many years now.

And would continue to be denied. He was accustomed to it, even if he sometimes longed for it more than anything else. When you didn't care for anyone or anything, didn't have that feeling of home, it couldn't be taken away from you. He knew from bitter experience it was better that way.

The bathroom door opened and Paige staggered out. When she saw him, she froze.

"You said you were leaving."

"I lied."

She came into the kitchen and grabbed a bottle of water out of the refrigerator. After she'd twisted off the top and took a gulp, she speared him with a glare. "You're good at that, aren't you?"

"I never lied to you, Paige."

"No, you just didn't tell me the truth," she snapped. Leaning against the counter, she took another sip of water as she eyed him.

"Actually I did," he said coolly. "I told you why I would keep you close if you worked for me."

She snorted. "I understood what you meant, but it wasn't the truth exactly. The truth would have been, 'Paige, I'm not really attracted to you, but I'd like you to think I am so you'll spill secrets about Chad's business. Then I'll steal his company and put you all out of work.'"

Her dark eyes were full of emotion. The anger and hatred he expected. But the fear?

Why should she fear him?

"I did not steal anything, Paige. What I did was acquire a failing company. And my attraction to you was not a lie."

She put a hand to her head, massaging her right temple. "Fine, you didn't steal anything and you really were attracted to me. I believe you. Now will you please go?"

He frowned as he watched her. "You need to sit down."

"I will once you've left."

"I'm not leaving just yet. Come, sit on the couch."

Her eyes were wide. "It's a way of life for you, isn't it? You just show up, snap your fingers and expect people to do your bidding. Well, I have news for you, mister—this is *my* home and no one jumps to your tune here. If you don't get out, I'm calling the police."

"If you sit down, I'll go." Her threat to call the police meant nothing to him, but clearly his presence agitated her. He'd done what he came to do. His body hummed with frustrated desire, but he tamped it down and ignored it. There was no reason to stay any longer than he already had. There was nothing for him here. Nothing for either of them.

"Fine," she said, coming around the counter and shuffling into the living room. She sank onto the couch, sighing almost wearily.

"You need a doctor," Alexei said, frowning. She still looked green and she was shaking.

"No, I'm fine." She bit her lip as she looked away. "I had the flu recently and I'm still recovering."

"Very well," he said. "Then I will leave you now. I left the coat on the chair in your foyer. Do what you wish with it, but do not send it back to me."

The phone on the counter began to ring, but Paige ignored it. Her head was tilted back, her eyes closed. She had a hand over her abdomen, and her skin was pale. He didn't want to go when she seemed sick, but she did not want him here.

He turned and strode down the small hallway. The answering machine kicked on. Paige's breathy voice asked the caller to leave a message. Did the woman have any idea she sounded like a phone sex advertisement?

The instant a cheery voice began to speak, Paige made a sound he'd never heard before. A sound of sheer panic. He could hear her lever herself up off the couch.

But she wasn't quite fast enough.

"This is Dr. Fitzgerald's office calling to confirm Paige Barnes's first ultrasound appointment for tomorrow at 1:00 p.m. You'll need to bring—"

Paige felt light-headed as she finished the call and put the receiver down. When the phone started ringing, she'd just been too tired to get up and answer it. All she wanted was for Alexei to go. She hadn't thought of her OB-GYN's office calling to remind her about an appointment she'd only made yesterday afternoon. Did they really think she could forget it in so short a time?

She looked up, knowing what she would see and afraid at the same time.

Alexei had come back down the hall. No, he had loomed back down the hall and now stood hulking nearby. His ice-gray eyes gleamed, his brows drawing down, his nostrils flaring as he stared at her.

"Why do you need an ultrasound, Paige?" He sounded cool, deadly, and a shiver dripped down her spine.

She thought about lying. But she couldn't think of a single reason anyone got an ultrasound other than pregnancy. She knew there had to be other reasons, but they escaped her.

She thrust her chin higher. Time to brazen it out. "Why do women usually get ultrasounds, Prince Voronov?"

What did it matter if she told him? He'd been cold enough to stage an elaborate seduction for the possibility of information that could benefit his precious company—and to hell with other people's lives and feelings—so why would he care about one tiny baby?

His eyes narrowed and she knew he was remembering, scrolling through the events of that night like it was a film he could view frame by frame. "You cannot be pregnant."

Oh, the arrogant bastard! "Why not? Because it wasn't part of the plan?" She tossed her head. "I assure you I *can*. But don't worry, I don't expect anything from you."

He didn't say anything for a full minute. Then he grabbed her by the shoulders and pulled her close, his face twisting in rage. And something else?

"You're lying. You cannot be pregnant with my child. We used protection."

Paige stared at him defiantly. "Of course I can't, because the great Prince Alexei Voronov has declared it impossible. So let me go and get the hell out of my house. We don't need you."

A wave of nausea hit her like a rogue wave storming the shore. She tried not to show it, tried so hard to be fierce and strong so he would just go away. But if the expression on his face was any indication, it didn't work.

"Paige, what's wrong? Tell me what's wrong."

She tried to jerk away, but it was like trying to escape iron manacles. "I'm pregnant, damn you, and if you don't let me go right this instant I'll throw up on your nice suit!"

He released her and she turned to dash for the bathroom, barely reaching the toilet in time. She could hear him behind her. She wanted to shut the door, shut him out, but she didn't have the strength.

Her hair lifted away and she realized he was holding her ponytail, keeping it out of the way while she retched. She was thankful for the gesture, and scared at the same time. Because it made her remember the Alexei who'd taken her for a *troika* ride, the haunted man who'd told her about his family lying in the crypt with such sadness in his eyes. The kind Alexei. The one she could have loved if he were real and not a careful construct.

But wasn't part of that construct really him?

Stop.

She just wanted him to leave her and never come back again. Seeing him hurt. It made her think of every moment they'd ever spent together, of that incredible few hours in his bed when she'd felt so alive and so feminine. He'd been her first real lover, and everything about it had been magical and beautiful.

But it had all been a lie. He'd ruined Chad, ruined Emma's happiness in the process, and she hated him for it. How could she ever let herself think of him with anything but contempt?

Because he was the father of her child and she felt a connection to him through the child they shared. A deep, mysterious connection that would forever be between them.

Dear God, why *him* of all people?

When she finished throwing up, when he helped her up and swooped her into his arms and carried her to the couch, she had no idea what would happen next. She expected nothing, yet she had to admit that she was relieved he'd come and relieved she'd told him the truth. She'd done the right thing. Mama would be proud of her for that, at least.

Emma was likely to never speak to her again, however. Since Paige had learned she was pregnant yesterday, she'd been dreading telling her sister. She'd certainly never intended to reveal who the father was, but she was afraid that choice had now been taken away.

"You need a doctor," Alexei said, whipping his phone from his pocket.

She was too tired to fight him. "This is normal, Alexei. Pregnant women get sick. Not all of them, but apparently I'm one. Lucky me," she finished on a whisper.

His eyes were hard, his expression determined. "You will need a doctor for the flight."

Alarm bells sounded in her head. "What flight? I'm not going anywhere. I have work to do, Emma's coming home in a couple of hours and we're watching a movie together on television tonight."

His handsome face was an impersonal mask. "I am leaving for St. Petersburg in two days. You are coming with me."

Paige tried to get up, but her stomach roiled in response. "I'm not going anywhere with you! My life is here."

"Not any longer. If this baby is truly mine, then your life is with me."

CHAPTER NINE

THE VORONOV PALACE was exactly as she'd last seen it, except that it was perhaps more beautiful now that spring had arrived. She'd never thought to see this place again. She'd certainly never thought to return as the new mistress of the manor. She glanced again at the three-carat rock on her right ring finger—Russians wore their rings on the opposite finger—and her insides squeezed tight.

She was married. To a prince.

And everything about this marriage was broken and wrong.

Paige let Alexei help her from the helicopter, then snatched her hand away as soon as she could do so. He showed no emotion at the defiant gesture. He'd been as cold as stone since the moment he'd informed her that she was coming to Russia with him.

She'd threatened to call the police, threatened to scream bloody murder, threatened him with any number of impotent gestures that he'd shrugged off as if they were nothing more than annoyances.

Which they had been. The all-powerful Prince Voronov could and would do whatever he wanted to do. Including ordering her life as if he had a right to do so. She'd been determined to resist, but he'd undercut all her protests with a single promise.

He'd promised to take care of Emma's future. Her tuition would be paid in full, and he'd buy her an apartment of her own—or the house they were living in if she wanted it. Emma would never have to worry for money again.

Paige had trembled at the choice, but she'd known what she was going to do from the moment he said it. She told herself that she hadn't refused because she was afraid of what the alternative would be. If Alexei could be gracious when he got his way, she imagined he would be formidable when he did not. She had only to think of what had happened to Chad and Russell Tech to know it was true.

So long as she lived, she would never forget Emma's face when her sister returned home that evening and saw Alexei in their house. She hadn't known who he was, but when he'd introduced himself, she'd recoiled as if he were evil incarnate.

And when Paige explained that she was pregnant, and the baby was Alexei's, she'd thought her sister would never get over the shock of betrayal. Emma began to cry, begging Paige to tell her it was a joke, that it couldn't be true, that she would never have done something so stupid and so wrong as to sleep with Chad's nemesis.

Paige had tried to explain, but Emma refused to listen. And then she'd run to her room and slammed the door. Paige had turned to Alexei, her eyes blurring with tears, and asked him if he was satisfied.

He'd been like a marble statue, cold and unfeeling. She'd wanted to claw his eyes out, to make him feel *something*. He'd merely watched her with those rain-cold gray eyes, awaiting her answer.

The next two days had been a whirlwind. Alexei had arranged for her to have an ultrasound that afternoon. He'd sat in the exam room stony-faced and silent. Until the technician began the process. Then he'd leaned in close, watching the monitor as if he were searching for the secret to eternal youth or something equally as precious.

Paige hadn't known she could get so emotional over the sight of a little tiny sac that contained nothing that resembled a baby in the least. But she had. She'd been flooded with wonder, protectiveness and overwhelming love. She'd been too scared to glance at Alexei, so she'd focused resolutely on the screen as the technician made a series of clicks on the computer. Her eyes had filled with tears. She should be here with a man who loved her, holding his hand while they saw their baby for the first time instead of with a cold stranger who disliked her.

"You're six weeks and three days exactly," the technician had finally said.

Alexei's sharp intake of breath was audible. And then he'd asked if she was sure. The technician had gone on to explain that pregnancies were dated from the date of the last menstrual cycle rather than the date of conception, and that yes, Paige was exactly six weeks and three days—which meant the date of conception was right around the time they'd been together.

Paige had wanted to die of embarrassment. He'd sounded as if he weren't certain he was the father and needed confirmation, which she imagined had caused the technician to explain as she had. Paige had felt as if he'd come right out and said she was a slut who slept around and that she was trying to fob off someone else's child as his.

What should have been a beautiful moment was ruined by his cold-blooded arrogance. Yet when she'd gotten up from the table, he'd reached out to steady her. And then he'd kept his hand on her back the entire way out to the car. His touch burned her like a brand and, in spite of her wish it was not so, her body reacted to him. Hot need softened her inner core, made her long to turn and bury her head against his chest.

She had not done so, of course. How could she want love and comfort from the man who'd stolen those things from her in the first place? Her life had been just fine, if a little boring, before he came along. And now he'd taken her sister and her home away. Her life would never be the same. But for the sake of her child, she would endure.

When they entered the palace, the same man who'd greeted them on that night a few weeks ago was waiting. He and Alexei exchanged a few words, and then he bowed and left. Alexei turned to her.

"Vasily is preparing a room for you. If you wish to wait in the drawing room, he will come for you when it is finished."

Paige locked her hands in front of her body. She was surprised they weren't sharing a room, but also somewhat relieved. How could she share a bed with him, knowing that her body craved his? The entire time she'd been standing next to him at the government office in St. Petersburg where they'd married, her body had been humming with electricity, and her mind had thrown images of the night they'd shared into her head.

She'd been determined to resist his sweet seduction when the time came, because she'd never imagined it would not.

But his announcement preempted her. Alexei was indifferent to her. She should have realized it considering the impersonal way in which he'd married her. Instead of a beautiful dress, flowers, happiness and friends, she'd been married in a sterile office by a public official who spoke a language she didn't comprehend.

"I want to know what happens now, Alexei."

She couldn't stand the uncertainty. What was she supposed to do as his wife? Were they going to live together as a couple, or would he leave her here and continue his life as it had been? There were so many things she didn't know, so many worries. She felt very far from home, and very out of her element. She felt as if her life had been stolen from her. A cold shot of fear dripped into her belly at the thought.

His arctic eyes glittered with heat. "You will go wait in the drawing room. There will be hot tea and a small lunch, if you can stomach it."

She bit the inside of her lip to keep from reacting to the thought of food. Her queasiness was getting better since the doctor had prescribed antinausea medication, but she still reacted sometimes.

"That's not what I meant and you know it," she said softly.

"Yes, but I have business to attend to and no time for chit-chat. You made a deal, Paige. If you are finding it difficult to keep up with your end of the bargain, then perhaps you would like me to reiterate the consequences if you do not?"

Her temper sparked. "I understand full well what you are capable of, Prince Voronov. How could I not?"

"And what does this mean? Have I been anything but kind to you, Paige? Have I neglected you or left you behind to raise my child alone?"

She stamped her foot in frustration, uncaring what he thought about the gesture. "I would have been perfectly happy to raise my baby without you. I don't need anything from you."

For the first time since she'd opened the door and seen him on her porch, a flash of emotion crossed his features. He took a step toward her. She would have backed away, except that she suddenly knew what a trapped rabbit must feel like. Safer not to move.

"Oh, yes, you had no plans to tell me about my child, did you? You would let him go through life without a father, when I could give him so much more than you ever could."

She sucked in a breath. He looked angrier than she'd ever seen him. The corners of his mouth were white, and she suddenly knew that what he'd been battling for the past two days—the reason he'd barely spoken to her—was anger.

How did he manage to make her feel petty and mean when he was the one who'd dragged her halfway around the world with him? The one who'd ruined everything with his greed? God, how she wished she'd never met him!

She tilted her chin up. "I didn't think you'd want to know."

It wasn't a good defense, but it was the truth.

His laugh was not friendly. It was a broken sound that ended before it began. "Because you know so much about me."

He punctured her indignation like a balloon, and her heart suddenly ached at the emotion behind his words. She was supposed to hate him, and yet she hurt for him. She'd been wrong to consider keeping the baby a secret, but she truly had believed he wouldn't be interested.

"I know nothing about you, Alexei," she said. "But I'd like to."

She was surprised to find she meant it. He was the father of her child—her husband—and she wanted to know him. They'd shared a beautiful evening once, even if it had all been a sham. Though it hurt to think of how he'd used her, she knew this was a consequence he had not foreseen.

His mouth opened, and she found herself leaning forward, wondering what he would say. Would this be a rapprochement for them? A new beginning? She was surprised at how badly she wanted it to be. She could learn—they both could—to put their animosity behind them for the sake of their baby.

But then Alexei's jaw snapped closed. He pivoted and strode down the hall.

* * *

Alexei felt as if he'd been standing beneath an oilrig when it had suddenly, and without warning, crashed down on top of him. He'd gone to Texas to examine his new acquisition and returned home with a wife.

A wife.

And not only a wife. From the moment he'd heard the voice of a nurse inform Paige about her ultrasound appointment, he'd known what lay down the road he was traveling.

She'd been a virgin. She was pregnant. He'd gone back over the night in his head, and he'd remembered the one thing he'd tried to forget. He'd fallen asleep beneath her, their bodies still joined. When he'd awakened, the condom was loose. It didn't take a genius to figure out how she'd gotten pregnant.

He'd been careless, and now he was suffering the consequences.

Alexei put his head in his hands. He couldn't concentrate on the figures in front of him any longer. He did not want a wife. He did not want a child. He'd already lost the people he'd loved, and he had no room to care for anyone again. It was not a risk he'd ever planned to take.

But already he felt a burgeoning protectiveness toward the child she carried.

And toward her.

Chert poberi!

She was a thorn in his side. She looked at him with those wide, dark eyes, with her emotions on her sleeve, and he wanted to take her in his arms and tell her it would be okay.

But it wouldn't be okay.

How could he say it would? He'd said the same thing to Katerina, yet they had both known the truth. He would not do it again. He would not put his heart and soul on the line for life to crush. It was easier being alone. He understood how to be alone.

He did not understand how to be a husband and father.

Then why didn't you leave her in Dallas?

He did not know why, except that he could *not* do so. She was carrying his child. He'd thought the Voronov line, the direct paternal line, would probably die out with him since each year passed without him taking a wife. But Paige had changed everything.

On the long flight home, when she'd curled up in the center of the big bed in his suite, he'd wanted to lie with her. He'd wanted to curl behind her, to pull her into the protective curve of his body and spread his hand over her abdomen. He'd wanted to feel her breathing, smell her summery scent and sleep beside her.

He'd done none of those things, though the impulse had been overwhelming. The thought of doing them horrified him. What was happening to him? How could he let one small woman get beneath his skin like this?

Alexei got to his feet. There was only one answer. He had to leave. He had to go somewhere else, had to leave her here at the Voronov Palace where she would be safe. She would grow big with their baby, and he would make sure she had the best care available.

But he would be elsewhere, running his business and building his empire even bigger and better than before. He would visit from time to time, make sure she was thriving, but he would not stay for long. And he would never touch her again.

Because he was afraid, if he did, he'd never want to stop.

"I have to return to Moscow on business."

Paige's head snapped up. She'd gone for a walk on the vast grounds of the palace and found a stone bench beneath an arbor. It was peaceful, beautiful. A cascade of pink roses spilled down the arbor, their blooms sweet and profuse. It was a vastly different landscape from a month ago. It had gone from wintery wonderland to spring garden in a short amount of time.

The air still had a slight chill. She'd worn a sweater, but her hot Texas blood was beginning to cool in spite of it. She was accustomed to a far warmer climate.

"Hello, Alexei," she replied.

He loomed beneath the arbor, hands shoved into his trouser pockets, his broody face closed and dark. Her heart skipped a beat as she watched him. No matter how hard she tried, she couldn't help but remember shoving his shirt from his body and running her hands over all that smooth, hard muscle.

"I will be gone a few days, but you will have everything you need. And if you do not, you have only to tell Vasily and he will see to it that you are taken care of."

Her heart had sped up while he talked. "You're leaving? So soon?"

She'd expected he would have to leave on business from time to time, but she hadn't expected it would happen within hours of their arrival. He was the only person she knew in this country. How could he leave her when everything about this situation was still so new? Who would she talk to? What would she do all day? She was used to working, used to taking care of herself. How was she supposed to do nothing at all?

She felt as if she were suffocating, as if she'd left one life where she'd been obligated to the needs of her sister only to step into another where she was at the whim of a man. A man who wouldn't want her if it weren't for the child in her body. Everything she'd ever wanted for herself, every dream and every scrap of independence, had been taken away from her by this enigmatic man.

And now he was leaving, as if it were nothing. As if she were nothing.

Alexei shrugged. "My business needs me."

"And you can't work from here for a few days? We've only just arrived."

He frowned down at her. "You cannot understand the pressures of my life."

Her spine stiffened. "Oh, really? I worked in the energy business for two years, Alexei. I understand the pressure that goes along with being a CEO. I did work for one, remember?"

He snorted. "But not a good one, *da?*"

Paige gritted her teeth. It was just like him to take a swipe at her ex-boss. "I like Chad. He was always good to me, he paid me very well, and he loves my sister."

"So you have forgotten his treatment of you."

Paige got to her feet. "His treatment? Chad never treated me wrongly, Alexei. I've told you that time and time again. In fact, I think he's treated me better than you have."

He took a step toward her, his brows drawing down. His face was a thundercloud. "He treated you so well that he lied to you about his affair with your sister. In fact, if I seem to remember, they *both* lied. And you put yourself in danger because of their lies."

"That's not what I was talking about," she said, her heart kicking up again.

"No, of course not. You forget that I helped you, that without me you would have been caught and abused by those men. But of course I am the one who has treated you wrongly."

Paige pulled a tendril of hair from her mouth where the wind had blown it. His gaze seemed to linger on her lips, his eyes darkening slightly before he looked away again.

"I thanked you for helping me that night. But you've not done a thing with my best interests in mind since. You've done what was best for *you.*"

His gaze whipped back to her. "Do you think marrying

you was best for me? That bringing you here is what I wanted to do?"

If he'd stabbed her in the heart with a jagged knife, he could have hurt her no worse. She knew he didn't want her. But to hear it stated so starkly?

She would not cry. She didn't need him. *They* didn't need him.

"You made that choice, Alexei, not I. If you regret it so much, then why don't you let me go home?"

"You are home," he snapped. "For the sake of the child, you are where you belong."

She folded her arms beneath her breasts, shook off a chill. "I sometimes wish we'd never met."

Something flashed across his face, but it was gone too quickly for her to be sure what it was. "It is too late for that. We must deal with the consequences of our actions as best we can."

She blinked. "The consequences of our actions? Is that how you think of this baby?" As if she hadn't thought the same thing herself. But he said it so coldly, without even a hint of emotion. Did he love this baby, or did he just feel obligated?

"He is a consequence, is he not?" He took a step closer. She thought he would reach for her, but he just stood there with his hands shoved deep in his pockets, his rainy eyes gleaming with heat.

"He might be a she," she said softly. Because she couldn't think of anything else to say when he stood so close. She could smell the subtle spice of his skin, could feel the heat emanating from him. Suddenly she wanted to slip her arms around his waist, press her cheek to his hard chest. *Why?*

"It doesn't matter," he said. "This baby is a Voronov, a royal descendent of my line, and I *will* protect him—or *her*—with every last breath in my body."

Paige trembled. Not because he'd frightened her, but because he was so fierce and she believed he meant every word. He would never let harm come to their baby. He was an honorable man. She believed it to her core.

But he was not honorable in everything. And that's what she didn't understand.

"I want to know," she said, drawing in a deep breath to steady herself, "why you destroyed Russell Tech. I want to understand."

She *needed* to understand, because if she didn't, the guilt of what she had done would eat her alive. How could she be his wife if she felt guilty every time her body responded to him?

She didn't think he would answer her. He would think she didn't deserve an answer, or he would tell her it was simply business. He'd done that once before. She expected it, waited for it, yet she'd still had to ask.

His gray eyes took on a faraway cast, as if he were looking at some distant object she could not see.

And then he spoke, his gaze coming sharply into focus once more. What he said rocked her to the core.

"Tim Russell destroyed my family. He took everything, and he didn't stop until nothing was left."

CHAPTER TEN

PAIGE'S KNEES FELT weak so she sank onto the bench again. Or fell onto it maybe. Alexei's face was stark, raw with emotion. She hadn't expected it, and her heart went out to him, squeezed tight in her chest with sympathy.

But what if he was wrong? What if he'd misunderstood?

She quickly dismissed that thought as ridiculous. How could he misunderstand something so important? He truly believed it, regardless of what she thought.

"I'm sorry," she said, because she didn't know what else to say.

He turned, his face in profile to her, and stared out at the vast gardens. "My aunt was a ballet dancer with the Bolshoi. She met Tim Russell when she was on tour with the company in the United States. They married a short while later."

Paige couldn't have moved if she tried. Alexei's aunt had been married to Chad's father?

"But that means…"

"That Chad is my cousin, yes."

"I've met his mother," she said softly. "I had no idea she was Russian."

And Chad had never mentioned the family connection. Why not? He'd briefed her about his nemesis on the flight to Moscow, but he'd never once said that Alexei was his cousin.

But she'd only been an employee. Why would she need to know the personal side of their story? She didn't. Yet knowing he'd been romancing her sister at the same time, she felt oddly betrayed once again that he had not told her this information.

Would it have changed her reaction to Alexei? Would it have made her more cautious when he professed an interest in her? Perhaps she would have realized just how brutal this feud was and kept above the fray.

As if that were an excuse, she chided herself. She'd known that Chad and Alexei were business rivals and she'd still let herself be charmed. What would knowing the true relationship have possibly done to make it different?

"Did you not ever wonder where he learned to speak Russian?" Alexei asked.

"I assumed he learned it in college." She stared at her clasped hands on her lap, heat rising into her cheeks. Was there absolutely anything she'd not been deceived about?

"He learned it from his mother, just as he learned to hate us from her as well."

"But why?" she asked, unable to fathom what would make Elena Russell do such a thing. She'd thought Chad's mother was a bit standoffish, but she'd never thought the woman was rude or hateful. The few times she'd been in the office, she'd been nice enough. She just hadn't been overly friendly. Paige had chalked it up to reserve. Some people were just that way.

His expression was like granite. "My father's family believed my mother too lowborn to deserve the title of princess, and that created a rift between them and us. When my father died, it was my grandmother who turned us out. She should not have been able to do so, but she knew people in certain places and my mother did not."

Paige's heart throbbed with feeling. How could anyone

throw her grandchildren out into the cold, even if she didn't like their mother? It was monstrous, unfathomable.

"Where does Chad's father fit into this?" she asked.

"When he was expanding his operations, Elena suggested he go to my mother and try to purchase the bit of land she'd gotten on my father's death. By then, the majority of the family property had passed into state hands with the death of my grandmother. All that was left was what my mother had."

Paige shook her head. "I'm not sure I understand."

"We had nothing, Paige." Alexei shoved his fingers through his hair. "Nothing except our land, and not much of it either. Russell made promises to my mother in exchange for her selling to him. It should come as no surprise that he kept none of those promises," he finished, his jaw so hard she thought it might crack.

"But he paid you money, right? Didn't that help some?"

He snorted in disgust. "He paid far less than he would make when he developed it. And when he struck oil, he refused to share any of the profits as he'd promised. My mother was too trusting, and we ended up with less than nothing."

So Chad's father had bought Voronov land, promised to give them a share of profits, then disappeared with the money. She could understand why Alexei would dislike the Russells. But as successful as he now was, did he really need to embark on revenge simply to get back at Chad's family for what they'd done?

Tim Russell was dead, and Alexei was beyond rich now. She hurt for him, but she also hurt for Chad. They were both victims of one man's greed, and it didn't seem fair to either of them. They had so much in common, if only they could see it.

"I think I understand why you wanted to acquire Russell Tech," Paige said. "But Chad's father died a long time ago.

Could the two of you not leave this in the past? You're *family*."

"*Nyet,*" Alexei spat. "Chad and his mother are nothing to me."

He ground his teeth together to keep from lashing out. How had he started on this trip down memory lane anyway? He had never, ever shared the details of what had happened so long ago with anyone.

And now he was spilling his guts to her as if they were two women gossiping about their lives. What was happening to him? He'd come out here to tell her he was leaving, because though he'd considered ordering the helicopter and simply going, he'd felt it was wrong to abandon her without an explanation.

Now he wished he'd done exactly that. He should have left and to hell with the rest.

She didn't understand, not really. He was surprised at how much he wanted her to. All he needed was to tell her the rest, to tell her about Katerina, and her lovely face would crease in sympathy. She might even get up and wrap her arms around him.

But he could not do it. He could not endure it if she touched him. And he found he couldn't speak the words about Katerina, couldn't say it aloud when he'd never done so before. No one knew that he'd gone to Dallas to beg for her life. No one knew that Tim Russell had laughed in his face and thrown him out. He'd been too humiliated to ever share it with anyone.

He would not start now.

"It is not as simple as that," he bit out.

"But what has Chad done to you?" she asked, her eyes shining with hope. As if she wanted him to see the error of his ways, wanted to play mediator and reunite him with the only branch of his family still living.

She'd boiled it down to a simple formula and she wanted

him to swallow the pill. It was so typically Paige that he would have laughed if he weren't raging inside. She'd spent her life pleasing people and did not see why everyone couldn't—or wouldn't—do the same.

"Chad inherited his parents' dislike of me along with Russell Tech. I assure you, had he been the one to close the Valishnikov deal, our situations would be reversed."

"I don't doubt that, but it doesn't need to be this way. It only takes one of you to change it. You should go to him, should talk—"

"Stop," he ordered, his voice harsh and full of the hatred he felt for the Russells. "Not everything can be fixed, Paige. Nor should it."

He didn't like the way she looked at him, the way her lovely dark eyes seemed so sad and disappointed and wary all at once. Again, she made him feel like a great Russian bear, ready to devour her whole and spit out the bones. It made him angry. He might not have been completely honest with her, but he'd never set out to harm her.

"You have no idea what you're talking about," he continued. "You think everything is simple, that a lifetime of problems can be solved with a conversation. You think that I need to forgive and forget, that I somehow need Chad and Elena because we share DNA."

"I never said that," she protested. "But I don't understand why you don't try. Someone has to make the first move."

"It will not be me," he said. "I don't need them. I don't need anybody."

Her eyes shimmered with hurt. "Of course you don't. It's much easier that way, isn't it? Needing people leaves you vulnerable."

He was so stunned he couldn't speak. He'd dated many women, but he'd never shared the details of his life with them. And even if he had, he knew in his bones that none of them would have seen what she had just now. She'd pierced the veil of his pride, of his loneliness, of his shield, and she'd stabbed into the soft heart of the matter.

It was easier not to need anyone. Easier not to love anyone. She saw through him, and he couldn't bear it a moment longer than he had to.

"I have to go now," he said stiffly. "There is much to be done before we are ready to develop Valishnikov's land. I will return as soon as I am able."

"Why can't I go with you? I don't know anyone here but you, and I don't want to be alone."

Her plea cut him to the bone. But he had to stand firm in this. He needed to get away from her until he could regain his perspective. "You will not be alone. Vasily is here, and the staff. There is much for you to do. You will need to learn Russian. When I return, there will be cocktail parties, dinners and evenings at the ballet and theater. You must learn to be a princess."

"Why can't I learn Russian in Moscow?"

"Because I wish you to learn it here."

Her expression fell just a little. "You don't really want me, do you, Alexei? You married me for the baby, just like you seduced me for information. *I* don't matter to you at all."

Isn't that what he wanted her to think? It was easier this way, easier than messy emotional entanglements. Not that he *was* emotionally entangled, but if he stood here and justified himself, if he tried to soothe her, he would only hurt her more. And he didn't want to do that.

When he found his voice, it was hard. Just like he needed it to be.

"You are my wife and the mother of my child. You are a princess, and wealthier than you have ever dreamed. What more could you possibly need from me?"

"What more indeed," she said, turning her head away to gaze into the distance just as he had earlier.

"I will return in a few days." He stood there a moment more, hesitating. For what reason, he did not know.

She waved a hand as if she were a queen dismissing a functionary. She did not look at him. "Fine. Have fun."

A few days turned into a week. A week turned into two. Paige had never felt so angry, so alone and so useless in her life. Alexei had dragged her to Russia, married her, and left her to rot in a gilded prison. This was not how she'd envisioned her life turning out. At only twenty-six, she'd thought she had a lifetime ahead of her to do what she wanted, to explore the world, to find a partner in life and get married. To have children.

Reflexively she pressed her hand to her abdomen. This child was the only wonderful thing about her relationship with Alexei.

But nothing about this life was normal. She'd left everything behind for the promise of financial security for her sister. But what about her needs? What about the baby? Would Alexei ever be more than a figurehead? Or would he simply leave phone messages and make vague promises about returning soon?

Paige had been deceived about so many things. Deceived about Chad and his relationship with Emma. Deceived about Alexei's true intentions when he'd first professed an interest in her. Deceived about the family connection between the man she worked for and the man she'd fallen into bed with.

Everything had been a deception. The only real thing in her life was this baby. Her fingers tightened over her belly. Sometimes she wondered if the baby was still there. How would she know? According to the doctor, she wouldn't show for some time, and she wouldn't feel movement for several more weeks.

"Please don't leave me, little one," she murmured. "You're all I have left."

The only person who would need her and love her was this baby. She hadn't heard from Emma since she'd left Texas two weeks ago. It tortured her to think that Emma might never forgive her.

And it angered her. Because she and Emma had been together so long and been through so much. How could her sister truly cut Paige from her life after all they'd been through? She knew Emma was angry, rightfully so, but Paige had to believe her sister would eventually pick up the phone or send an e-mail.

Because if she didn't believe it, she would never make it through the endless days and nights.

And the days literally were endless. This far north, it never got fully dark at night. As the solstice approached, the sky darkened to dusk, and the horizon stayed pink until the sun rose only a few short hours later. It was beautiful and magical, and yet there was no one to share it with.

Paige was more alone here than she'd ever been in the darkest, loneliest hours after her mother had died.

It was true there was a large staff at the Voronov Palace, but they were here to serve her, not to be her friend. Not that she hadn't tried to make friends, but Vasily frowned upon it. He was formal and structured. He bowed in her presence and called her "princess," no matter how odd it made her feel.

She did not feel like a princess, but he insisted on maintaining that level of formality and he insisted the staff do so as well. She'd been assigned a personal assistant, a cool young woman named Mariya whose job it was to transform her into a princess worthy of Alexei. So far, there had been daily Russian lessons, etiquette lessons and deportment lessons.

Today, Mariya had informed her, they were going on a shopping trip to St. Petersburg. Paige, who had never been comfortable shopping in her life, looked forward to the trip as if it were her favorite thing to do. Finally a chance to get out of the palace and see *something*.

The ride into town took about a half an hour. Mariya sat silent and respectful across from Paige in the limo, only speaking when Paige asked questions or commented on the sights. Another dark car led the way in front of them, with a following car behind them.

"Why do we need three cars?" Paige asked.

Mariya regarded her evenly. "It is security, your highness."

"Security?" She'd given up asking Mariya not to call her *your highness*. "Is it dangerous where we are going?"

Mariya's short blond hair didn't dare to move a millimeter when the woman shook her head. "You are a princess and your husband is very wealthy. Security is appropriate."

When they arrived on the Nevsky Prospekt, where all the couture boutiques were located, Mariya made Paige wait in the car while she had a security team check each store before they went inside. Once the men gave their okay—what manner of sinister things they expected in a clothing store, Paige had no idea—Mariya hustled Paige into the building.

Once inside, a team of women descended. Mariya conversed with them in Russian, and then Paige was whisked into the back of the shop and dress after dress was brought out for her inspection. Because she didn't know the first thing about fashion, she ended up saying they were all nice. Finally, Mariya gave a crisp order and several of the garments were taken away.

"Please try these on, Princess Voronova," she said.

Paige spent the next hour trying on clothes and shoes. When she emerged in a wine-colored silk gown, another woman was standing there, a frown fixed on her face. Mariya, Paige noted, seemed irritated.

"Princess Voronova, may I introduce you to the Countess Kozlova?"

"So this is the American that Alexei has married," the countess interjected with a sniff.

Something about the way the woman said Alexei's name sent a spear of jealousy through Paige's breastbone. That, and the other woman's appearance. The countess was blonde and groomed to within an inch of her life. She exuded elegance and poise, and she looked far more like the kind of woman Alexei should be with. She made Paige feel duller and frumpier than she ever had.

It surprised her, but the thought of Alexei with another woman had the power to make her crazy. He was still such a stranger to her, and yet she sometimes felt as if they were connected by more than just a baby.

She felt foolish for thinking so, when clearly he did not feel compelled to return to her side. For all she knew, he was living the single life in Moscow, sleeping with a different woman every night and never planning to return to his plain, pregnant wife.

"Ochen' priyatno," Paige said.

The countess's exotic eyes narrowed. *"Mnye tozhye."*

Paige knew it was the proper reply, yet she doubted very much the countess was actually pleased to meet her. The problem with learning Russian was that she couldn't understand inflections the way she would if the woman had replied in sarcastic English.

"You must come to my salon," the countess said. "There are many people who would like to meet you."

Paige didn't know what to say. She glanced at Mariya, but the woman was busy staring at her feet. Instinctively she was certain the Countess Kozlova did not like her. But she wasn't certain she could refuse an invitation. Would it reflect badly on Alexei? Did she care if it did?

Paige felt a slow flush creeping up her neck. For God's sake, the man had left her alone since they'd returned from Texas. He'd told her to learn how to be a princess, and then he'd abandoned her instead of helping her to learn the role himself. She was out of her element, out of her depth and growing more furious by the minute.

How dare he throw her into shark-infested waters to sink or swim on her own! How dare he drag her from her life and those she loved when he didn't want or need her!

Was this how she was going to live? Was this how she was going to be the best mother for her baby? By cowering and moping and waiting for instruction?

Something inside her snapped as she faced the woman watching her so confidently, one immaculately groomed eyebrow lifted in question. She felt as if the countess was mocking her, as if the world was mocking her.

And she was sick of her lack of control over her own life.

By God, from now on she would stop living like a hermit in a grand palace and immerse herself in the life and culture. Alexei wanted a princess? Then he would get one, though it might not be the one he wanted.

"Speciba," she replied, lifting her chin. "I would be pleased to attend."

The countess bared her teeth in a smile. "Very well. I will send the details to your social secretary, *da?* I *so* look forward to it, Princess."

Countess Kozlova lived in a grand town house located on one of the canals that crisscrossed St. Petersburg and gave it the nickname "Venice of the North." On the drive into town, Paige had begun to believe she'd made a mistake in agreeing to come to the countess's party. Mariya hadn't said a word, but Paige could feel her assistant's disapproval.

She'd steadfastly ignored it, just as Alexei had ignored her. Three days had passed since she'd gone shopping and met the countess, and Alexei had not called once. Though Paige had wanted to pull the covers over her head and pretend she'd not accepted the invitation, she'd known she could not do so. Instead, after consulting Mariya as to the type of party this was and what she was expected to wear, she'd chosen a white silk gown and tall, crystal-studded sandals that peeked from beneath the hem whenever she walked.

A maid twisted her hair up into an elegant French knot, and then Mariya had shown up with a selection of jewels that made Paige's breath catch in her chest. The diamonds, Mariya had informed her, had once belonged to a Romanov queen. As if the glittering jewels weren't enough, Mariya had also produced a tiara.

Paige had stared at herself in the mirror for several minutes, her eyes glassing over with tears. She looked elegant, like a princess should look. For the first time since she'd come to Russia, she felt as if she might actually learn to belong here.

Appropriately gowned and coiffed, Paige had set out on the journey into town, her heart thrumming like a bird in a cage. Now, as she stood in the glittering ballroom surrounded by men and women speaking Russian, she once more felt alone and isolated and completely out of her depth.

She should not have come. She should have contented herself with a book like she had so many other nights. Mariya was by her side to translate, but unless the woman sat behind her at dinner and told her which fork to use when, Paige would be lost. There hadn't been much use for this kind of complicated etiquette where she'd grown up.

"Ah, Princess Voronova," the countess said as she sauntered

up with her hand wrapped around a man's arm, "it is so nice to see you. I wish you to meet my brother, Yevgeny. He has admired you from afar and I have said I would introduce you."

Paige hoped her palms weren't sweating too badly as she held out her hand. "Pleased to meet you."

Yevgeny bowed over her hand as he placed a kiss on the back of it. "Very beautiful," he murmured. "Perhaps you will honor me with a dance?"

"I'm not much good at dancing, I'm afraid," Paige said.

"Nonsense."

"No, it's true. There wasn't much time for dancing back home."

"Home is Texas, no?" the countess said. She turned to her brother. "Alexei is so amusing. When I saw him in Moscow a few days ago, he told me he'd married an American girl with no money or connections. Were you a cowgirl, Princess Voronova?"

The blood pounded in Paige's temples. This woman had seen Alexei recently? Had talked with him? He had spoken to her of their relationship?

"You have me at a disadvantage, Countess," Paige said as coolly as she could. "I've heard nothing at all about you from my husband."

The countess laughed, her golden eyes sparkling with a hint of malice. "No, I rather doubt you have. It might not be good for marital felicity, no?"

Before Paige could manage a reply, the countess turned to her brother and gave him a playful little slap on the arm. "Yevgeny, do be good to the princess, will you? I have to speak with Mr. Kaminski."

"My sister is angry with you," Yevgeny said once the countess was gone.

Paige watched the woman move across the room, her hips

rolling sensually as she walked, the curve of her buttocks swaying with the kind of practiced grace that Paige knew she did not have. Men's heads turned to watch her progress.

"I don't know why. I've done nothing to her."

He took her arm and began to lead her around the crowd toward a door on the other side of the room. Paige didn't want to be rude, so she didn't protest. But when she glanced behind her for Mariya, the woman had disappeared.

"Ah, but you have done something," he said smoothly. "You have married Prince Voronov, which is a task she had set for herself after the count died."

"I imagine if Alexei had wanted to marry her, he would have done so. It's hardly my fault."

Yevgeny laughed. He was tall, blond and rather handsome. He was the kind of man she used to be attracted to, she thought wistfully. But since Alexei had come into her life, she seemed to only want dark, brooding men who ignored her.

Yevgeny appeared to be nice enough, in spite of his sister, and his English was good. For the first time in weeks, someone was talking to her as an equal. It'd been too long since she'd had a normal conversation with anyone—though this was hardly a normal conversation.

"Yes," Yevgeny said, "she had her chance to reel him in when they were lovers."

Paige stumbled, but Yevgeny righted her. "Sorry," she said. Alexei and the countess had been lovers? Were they lovers when he'd taken her to the Voronov Palace that night so many weeks ago? Her temples throbbed with the notion. She'd known Alexei wasn't celibate when they'd met, but she'd never considered he was involved with someone else at the time.

Yevgeny had guided her onto a terrace that overlooked a canal. The sky was pink with the setting sun that would never entirely disappear for the night. A boat glided along the canal while people stood at the railings, watching the city slide by.

Yevgeny's hand skimmed her arm. "No, it is I who am sorry. You did not know my sister and your husband were lovers, and I have blurted it out."

Paige subtly pulled away from him. She was beginning to doubt that he was nice after all. "It's not your fault."

"Yet I feel responsible."

Paige wrapped her arms around her torso and shook her head. "No, really, you shouldn't. I'm sure there are many women in Alexei's past."

"Are you cold?"

"A little," Paige admitted. "I'm not used to this climate."

Yevgeny shrugged out of his jacket. "Here, let me help you," he said as he stepped behind her to settle the coat on her shoulders. She felt she should refuse, and yet she didn't want to be rude when he was simply being solicitous.

But when his hands lingered on her shoulders before sliding down her arms, a thread of panic unwound in her belly. She started to turn and tell him she wanted to go back inside.

"Isn't this cozy?" a voice growled. Paige's head whipped around as the dark shape in the door coalesced into a tall man in a tuxedo.

Relief flooded her. "Alexei? What are you doing here?"

His gray eyes gleamed with suppressed fury as he stepped closer. "You were not expecting me, I take it?"

CHAPTER ELEVEN

ALEXEI WANTED TO KILL the man standing so close to his wife. Yevgeny Petrov shot him a malevolent grin over the top of Paige's head, but it was Paige who held Alexei's attention. She was radiant, more beautiful than he remembered, and he wanted her with a fierceness that clawed his insides into ribbons.

Not a day had gone by that he hadn't thought about her, but he'd stayed away because he'd believed it was best for them both. Now that he was here, however, he realized it had been a mistake. She was too lovely and too vulnerable to leave her alone with predators like Petrov circling around.

He closed the distance between them and yanked her from Yevgeny's grip. She stumbled against him and he caught her close, trapping her in the curve of his arm.

"Stay away from my wife," he growled.

"Then perhaps you should keep her close," Yevgeny said in Russian.

Alexei pulled the jacket from Paige's shoulders and threw it at the other man. "Get out of my sight, Petrov."

Yevgeny took his time shrugging into his jacket. Then he bowed to Paige. "It was lovely to meet you, Princess Voronova," he said in English.

"I enjoyed talking with you, too," she said in that slight

Texas drawl, all Southern politeness and grace. "Thank you for your kindness."

Alexei waited until Yevgeny had passed into the house before he turned Paige in his arms.

"You are never to be alone with that man again, do you understand?"

"I'm surprised you care," she flung at him, her brows two sharp slashes in her face as anger replaced the politeness.

"You are my wife," he ground out. "Of course I care."

She snorted. "Really? And here I'd thought I was simply your prisoner. Or is this how wives are treated in Russia?"

He hadn't expected her anger, hadn't expected her to challenge him. It surprised him, fueled the fire in his veins. He hauled her closer, his temper on a gossamer string. "We are leaving now," he growled. "And you will never set foot in this house again."

A flash of discomfort crossed her features. "You're holding me too tight. You'll leave bruises."

He immediately released her. The last thing he wanted to do was hurt her. He took a step back, raked a hand through his hair. He'd barely spent three minutes in her company and already she made him lose control.

But seeing her with Petrov had made him crazy. She was too good for a snake like Yevgeny Petrov.

Not only that, but she was also his wife. Pregnant with his child. His gaze slipped to her belly, but she looked the same as she had nearly three weeks ago.

But when he met her eyes again, he amended the thought. She did not look the same. She looked...elegant. Beautiful and ethereal—and brimming with temper.

He didn't like her this way.

Or, he did like it, but he didn't like everyone else seeing what he saw. His Paige wore dull suits and glasses. This Paige was gowned in pure white, like a virgin or an angel. The silk skimmed her curves like water flowing over a creek bed. Her dark hair was pinned up, showing the graceful curvature of her neck. He recognized, with a flash of surprise, the Voronov diamonds at her throat. The tiara she wore had once been his great-great-grandmother's.

His body throbbed with heat and desire. He wanted to sweep her up and take her from this place right now.

"Where are your glasses?" he demanded.

She looked at him like he'd lost his mind. Which, he feared, he had.

"I'm wearing contacts. Are you going to tell me what you're doing here, Alexei, and why you're acting so bossy?"

He took his jacket off and wrapped it around her, belatedly remembering that she'd been cold. He'd stood in the entry and watched her with Yevgeny for several minutes before he'd interrupted. He didn't know why, except that maybe he'd wanted to see how she would react. Now, he felt small and petty for having done so. Paige had been innocent when he'd made love to her, and though she'd harbored a crush on Chad Russell, she'd never acted upon it.

But he'd stood there, watching Petrov, who was more like Chad in type than he was, and wondering what she would do if the man tried to kiss her. Except that he'd been unable to let it go that far.

"I could ask the same of you."

She blinked. "Without the bossy part, I assume. And I was invited."

"So was I."

"Do you mean you didn't know I would be here tonight?"

"I knew," he clipped out. Because Mariya had called to inform him of the fact. And he'd raced from Moscow because he could not stay away. "But I want to know why you came."

She pulled his jacket around her body, covering the dress. "Because I'm bored, Alexei, and tired of being alone. Because someone invited me to a party, and I wanted to be out among people, where there was laughter and music and conversation. I married you for our baby and for my sister's future, but I didn't agree to be your prisoner."

An erotic image of her bound to his bed with silken ropes flashed into his mind.

"You are not a prisoner," he said.

She snorted. "No, but I might as well be. If I'd known we weren't going to make a life together for the sake of our baby, I could have stayed in Texas and you could just visit whenever you found yourself passing through."

"Your life is here now. With me."

She stomped her foot. He'd noticed she often did so when aggravated. For some reason, he found it amusing. But he did not dare to smile now that she was bristling like a cat.

"But my life *isn't* with you! It's in your palace, where everyone is so cold and formal and no one talks to me like I'm a normal person!" She slapped a hand against her chest. "But I *am* a normal person, Alexei. I'm not a princess, not an exalted being—I'm just Paige Barnes from Atkinsville, Texas, and I don't know how to be anyone else!"

He reached for her hand. He'd been handling this badly, and it was time to regroup.

She snatched it away and crossed her arms beneath her breasts. The movement lifted the creamy swells, drew his gaze. He wanted to touch her, wanted to strip her and explore every last inch of her glorious skin.

"You are Princess Paige Voronova, and I don't want you to be anyone else," he said.

Her eyes glittered. "That's not how it looks from where I'm standing," she said, her voice almost a whisper.

Alexei sensed a softening in her and reached for her again.

This time she did not resist as he pulled her gently closer. He tipped her chin up. He had to kiss her. It had been too long, and he was suddenly dying to do so. Dying to see if the flame inside him whipped higher, or if it was all his imagination.

He lowered his head slowly, waiting to see what she would do. For a moment, he thought she would reject him, but then her eyes closed and her mouth parted.

A fierce surge of possession went through him. He hadn't expected her to surrender. The gesture stunned him, humbled him. He did not deserve her surrender, but he would not reject it. Not this time.

He hovered above her mouth, not kissing her just yet, but letting his gaze brush over the cream of her skin, the long sweep of her lashes where they fanned against her cheeks, before finally settling on the lush pink of her lips.

She was in that moment the most desirable woman he'd ever known.

Her eyes fluttered open in question, but before she could speak and puncture the wonder of it, he crushed his mouth down on hers. He had not kissed her since the night he'd made love to her, and the moment their tongues met, he wondered why in God's name not.

She clutched the lapels of his tuxedo, opened herself to him while he plundered the depths of her lush mouth. Alexei surrendered to the feeling. He was through fighting her pull on him. It was ridiculous to do so when he couldn't even imagine touching another woman. She was a fever in his blood that would not be abated through deprivation.

Tonight, he was taking her to his bed and to hell with anything else.

Paige hardly recognized the man who hurried her to the waiting limo and climbed in beside her. With a sharp command to the driver, he hit the button for the privacy glass before turning to her.

Her heart raced, but whether it was from the look in his eyes or the way he'd kissed her, she wasn't certain.

"I want you," he said as he pushed her back on the long, plush seat and spread his body over hers. "It has been too long."

Paige swallowed as the hard lines of his body pressed into her soft curves. She ached with heat and need, and though part of her gibbered that she shouldn't fall into his arms so easily, she knew she was ultimately going to do so.

His lips found the tender skin of her neck, and she sighed helplessly. How could she reject this pleasure?

There was something about this man, something about the way she felt when he touched her, that she could not deny. He turned her inside out, made her skin seem too tight and thin to contain what she felt for him.

Was this what it felt like to be in love?

Love. The word cracked in her brain like thunder over the Gulf of Mexico. How many times had she cowered from the power of those sonorous blasts as a child? She wanted to cower now, to hide her head in the sand and make the noise go away.

Love.

She could not love him. She didn't know him well enough, even if her heart insisted that she knew everything she needed to know. He was driven and strong and he felt things deeply. And he'd made her his wife because he would never abandon his child.

But there was still the matter of his deception. He'd set out to seduce her with a goal in mind. He'd not actually asked her for information that night, but she told herself it was because he'd learned what he needed during his endless phone calls instead.

"You are thinking about something," he murmured against her cheek.

It surprised her that he knew. "Yes."

"Tell me what it is."

"I'm wondering why you're here."

"I'm here because you are my wife."

She settled her palm on his cheek because she could not help but do so. He turned into her hand, kissed her skin. "I want to believe that," she said.

"Then believe it."

Her pulse throbbed in her throat, her temples. "I can't."

His gaze clouded. "What is this all about, Paige?"

"What's it *about?* How can you ask me that? You know what it's about!"

He sat up with a sigh. She scrambled into a sitting position. Part of her was cursing herself for opening her mouth, and another part was urging her on.

"I wish to make love to you, and you wish to talk." He shoved his fingers through his hair. "Yet I suppose I deserve it."

"I haven't heard from you in three weeks," she said. "And now you're here, kissing me and scrambling my brain—"

"I scramble your brain?" He looked supremely satisfied.

She folded her arms as if to shield herself. "You know you do. If you didn't, I doubt we'd be here now. I would not be pregnant, and you wouldn't have had to marry me."

He was moving toward her again, sliding her back against the seat once more. "I am liking this idea that I make you forget yourself," he purred.

She put her hands against his shoulders, though she did not push him away. "You do, and now you're making me forget that I'm upset with you. You left me all alone in a strange country with no friends, not to mention dragging me from my home in the first place. And you tried to seduce information out of me."

He kissed her throat. "I did not try to seduce information out of you," he murmured. "I intended to do so, but I forgot all about it in my desire to bed you."

Her eyes closed and she bit back a moan. *Concentrate.* "Is that supposed to make me feel better?"

"I don't see why not." He flexed his hips against her, his glorious hardness pressing into her sensitive core. "This does not lie, *maya krasavitsa.* I wanted you then and I want you now. But I am sorry I hurt you."

"Are you really?"

He lifted his head and gazed down at her. The expression on his face was intense, solemn. "*Da,* I am. I should have never attempted to use your connection to Chad."

She couldn't say why precisely, but she believed him. She simply knew it in her soul that he meant what he said. Her heart swelled until she hurt from the intensity. "Thank you. It means a lot to hear you say it."

"I am not perfect, Paige, but I admit when I am wrong."

He lowered his head to kiss her again, but Paige braced a hand against his chest. "One more thing."

One eyebrow arched in question.

Paige swallowed. But she would not be stopped. She deserved to know. "I want to know what your relationship with the countess is."

He answered without hesitation. "She was my mistress very briefly, and that was quite some time ago."

"You were not with her when we were first together?"

"No."

"She said she saw you in Moscow recently. You told her about me."

He grinned, and her heart flipped. "And you would prefer I kept you a secret?"

"That's not what I meant."

"Countess Kozlova is a vain, shallow woman," he said. "She means nothing at all to me, and never has. Does this satisfy you?"

"I'm not sure," she said. "How do I know you're telling me the truth?"

He looked suddenly very serious. "Because the truth, Paige, is that I have not been with another woman since the night I was with you."

She was stunned into temporary speechlessness. "But—but...I saw you. That actress—"

He flexed his hips and sent a current of sensation arcing through her body. "She was quite disappointed, I assure you."

He lowered his head, his lips touching hers gently, a light skimming of flesh against flesh. "I have been unable to think of anything but that night we shared, the night we created a baby," he murmured. "There has been no one but you since that night."

Tears pressed against the backs of her eyes. It was so close to what she wanted to hear from him, and yet not close enough. But how could she reject him now? How could she say no when this was a beginning? It was possible, wasn't it, that they could build a relationship together if only they tried?

Suddenly she wanted more, wanted to feel if he was real and this moment not simply a figment of her imagination. Would she wake soon, hot and throbbing and disappointed?

She wasn't sure who deepened the kiss first, but it soon turned erotic, sizzling, a meeting of lips and tongues and teeth that was so deep and thorough Paige thought she might combust at any moment. And then his hand skimmed down her silk-clad form until he reached her ankle.

He caught her hem, inched her dress up, his fingers sliding

over her calf, along the inside of her knee, her thigh. Paige whimpered as his thumb brushed across the silk of her panties. Sparks of sensation ignited in her belly as moisture pooled between her thighs.

"Alexei—"

"No more words, Paige. Just feel. Just enjoy."

When he sat up and removed her panties, she could only hold her breath and wait for what he would do next. Did he truly intend to make love in the confines of the car as it moved through the city? The idea was wicked, exciting. She felt as if she should protest, and yet she craved his touch. She wanted to see what he would do next, wanted to feel every sensation he could give her. It'd been too long since she'd felt close to anyone, and she longed for the contact. Deprivation had made her reckless, she decided.

But when he slid his hands beneath her buttocks, she instinctively closed her legs. Was it modesty or fear? She wasn't certain. Without a word, Alexei eased her thighs open and settled between them. Paige held her breath, her heart thundering in her ears with anticipation.

The instant his mouth touched her hot center, her back arched off the seat and she gasped out his name.

He was relentless, bringing her to stunning climax again and again until she begged him to stop. Her body was so sensitized that she couldn't take any more.

But she wanted more. She wanted him, inside her, taking her to the heights of sensation with nothing but skin and heat between them.

She wanted him with a hunger she'd never imagined possible.

Alexei pulled her dress back down and settled into the seat beside her as if nothing had happened. She lay against the door frame, her chest heaving, her body singing, and felt disappointment seep through her that he had not continued.

"What about you?" she asked when she could manage to string two words together.

His silver eyes glittered, the corners of his delicious mouth turning up in a wicked grin. "Do not worry, *maya krasavitsa,* this night is far from over."

As if he'd planned it to the second, the car rolled to a stop. Paige sat up and smoothed her dress before the door could open. A moment later, the chauffer held the door while Alexei helped her out of the car.

"But this is a hotel," Paige said as they walked through the glass carousel into the soaring lobby.

"*Da.* I keep a suite here, for when I need to be in the city."

He led them over to a private elevator and slipped a card through the reader. When the door opened again, it was onto a suite decorated in sleek cherry and steel, sparkling glass and plush leather.

Alexei swept her into his arms and carried her over the threshold. It was romantic, but she told herself not to read anything into it. It was impatience, not romance, that had him carrying her into the bedroom and setting her on the floor before he located the hidden zipper at the side of her gown.

Their clothes disappeared in quick fashion, and then they were tumbling onto the bed and Alexei was thrusting into her body. There was nothing between them this time, no barrier, and the sensation was exquisite. His hard flesh fit her so perfectly that a tear slipped down her cheek.

It was only the second time they'd made love, and yet it felt as if they knew each other's bodies as intimately as lovers of a dozen years. They moved in tune, as a single entity, his thrusts matching hers, until the explosion that happened was so exquisite, so extraordinary, that they both cried out with the power of it.

Afterward, they lay tangled together, their bodies sweating, their breaths cooling their skin, and let their hands wander over each other.

"You are extraordinary," Alexei said sometime later.

Paige sighed contentedly. She didn't feel extraordinary. She felt…peaceful, as if she'd been swirling in a vortex and had finally landed on solid ground. "I feel very ordinary," she replied, yawning.

Alexei toyed with her nipples. Sharp, sweet sensation spiked through her, pooling in her core.

"Your breasts have grown bigger," he said softly.

"They are more sensitive, too."

"I had noticed this."

She pushed back until she could look him straight in the face. "How could you possibly know that? We don't exactly have a long history together."

"No, but what we do have is imprinted on my brain. I have a memory for these kinds of things."

"I'll just bet you do," Paige grumbled.

His brows drew down. "What does this mean?"

"It means that I wonder how well you remember what turns Countess Kozlova on."

He laughed suddenly, startling her. "Jealous, Paige? I have told you she means nothing to me."

"Of course I'm not jealous," she said, though the blush creeping beneath her skin gave away the lie.

Alexei's hand slid to her belly, caressing her. She imagined what it would feel like when she was bigger and the baby could kick in response.

He looked up, his silver eyes intense as they caught and held hers. "I have no desire for any woman but you."

Paige pulled the sheet up, shielding her body as if she could also shield her heart. It was what she wanted to hear from him, and yet it frightened her as well.

Alexei frowned. "What is the matter, Paige?"

"I'm just wondering when the fairy tale ends." Because it would. Just like the last time, the bottom would drop out and she'd find it had all been a lie.

"Don't fairy tales always have a happy ending?" he said lightly.

"Not if you're the wicked witch."

He laughed. "Surely you are not trying to tell me you're the wicked witch?"

Paige couldn't help but smile even as she tried to be serious. "Of course not. I was just trying to say that it all depends on your perspective. The fairy tale might not always end well."

In a quick movement, he stripped the sheet back and moved on top of her, his body hovering over hers, hard and warm and sexy. Paige's breath caught in her throat as her desire quickened inside her again.

"It's our fairy tale," he breathed, his mouth finding the hollow of her throat. "We get to write how it ends."

Paige arched her neck and moaned at the exquisite sensation of his lips moving over her collarbone, between her breasts. Her heart swelled for him, swelled with all she was beginning to feel. She wanted the fairy tale and she wanted the happy ending.

And she wanted tonight. She wanted him like this always, as starved for her as she was for him. She didn't want to think it could end, though she knew it could. But tonight she would not consider it.

He placed a reverent kiss on her stomach before working his way back up her torso. She could feel him between her legs, hard and ready, and her insides liquefied. How did he do this to her? How did he make her feel as if she could never get enough of him?

"You must tell me if it's too much, if you are too tired," he said.

Paige tilted her hips up, sliding her calves along his thighs to hug his waist. "Make love to me, Alexei."

When he entered her this time, it was without the urgency of before. He made love to her slowly, sweetly, taking her to the heights and then bringing her gently back to earth with the exquisite pressure of his body inside hers.

She hadn't known he could be so tender and in control, hadn't known it could be even more beautiful between them than it already had been. As she lay in his arms after, drifting into sleep, she feared her heart was already lost.

CHAPTER TWELVE

PAIGE RETURNED FROM a stroll on the grounds of the palace to find Alexei standing on the terrace, hands shoved in the pockets of the khakis he was wearing, lost in thought. She stopped beside the stone steps leading up to the terrace and watched him.

He was still so breathtaking, and he made her heart thrum with excitement just looking at him. His handsome face was in profile to her. He shoved a hand through his dark hair and lifted the drink he was holding with the other. She wanted to ask him what was wrong, but she sensed that he would not welcome the intrusion.

In the weeks since he'd burst into the Countess Kozlova's salon and whisked her away, they'd spent the days talking, making love, eating dinner on the terrace or beside the fire on cool evenings and taking small trips into town to see the sights.

He'd taken her for a cruise on the Neva River, shown her the Hermitage Museum and the Admiralty, St. Isaac's Cathedral, and the Peter and Paul Fortress on Zayachy Island, among other things. He'd explained that the spire of the St. Peter and Paul Cathedral was the tallest structure in the city, but when he'd asked if she wanted to go up on the viewing platform, she'd refused. Alexei had laughed and hugged her.

"I do not blame you, *lyubimaya moya*. It is very high."

They'd spent a few evenings at the ballet and opera, as he'd promised. Her Russian was getting better, though she could in no way be called fluent. But she'd enjoyed the opera regardless. Mariya had delivered librettos in English, and Paige had read them through before attending in the evening.

Watching Alexei now, she put a hand over her belly. She was nearly fourteen weeks along, and though she couldn't feel movement yet, they had seen their baby on the ultrasounds. It was too early to know if they were having a girl or a boy, but all she had to do was think of that little fist pumping in the air during the ultrasound, and she melted with love.

Paige was humbled by the love she felt for this child. She loved her sister, and she'd worked hard to make a good life for them both, but she'd never felt the kind of protective possessiveness she felt toward this baby growing inside her. It was an experience in a whole new realm.

She wanted to share what she was going through with Emma, but they were so far apart now—both literally and figuratively. Emma had finally e-mailed her, and they'd spoken on the phone several times, but the chill had not completely dissipated. In some ways, it made her angry, but in others she understood.

She'd done everything for Emma for the last eight years, and now she was halfway around the world, married to the man who'd destroyed Emma's fiancé. It was awkward, and yet it hurt her that Emma couldn't find it in herself to understand what Paige was going through. Her entire life had changed when she'd fallen pregnant with Alexei's child, and she was doing the best she could to make something good and lasting in her new life.

It wasn't what she'd once thought would happen to her, but each day she spent with Alexei, she knew it was the right thing. The fairy tale would end the way she wanted it to. She refused to let it happen any other way.

Once, when she'd spoken of her sister's lack of support to Alexei, he'd asked her why she wasn't angry that Emma's first thought the day Paige had told her the news was how it affected *her*.

"She did not ask how you were feeling, Paige, or if the baby was well."

"She was upset," Paige defended.

"Yes, but if the situation were reversed, you would have been more concerned for her welfare than for your own."

She'd known he was right, even if she couldn't admit it. And that's what hurt the most. Emma *had* been more concerned about herself—and still was, to a certain extent.

Paige pushed away the sadness that accompanied her thoughts of Emma and watched her husband in silence. A slow, steady warmth trickled into her veins. Her body always hummed when he was near. It was desire, yes, but she knew it was more than that.

Life with Alexei had been almost perfect these last weeks. He was attentive to her every need, gentle when she wanted it, and fierce when she needed him to be. He knew her so well, sometimes better than she knew herself. It was stunning, really.

One of his smiles had the power to rock her world to its very foundations. She woke up in his arms each morning, and fell asleep in them each night, and she couldn't imagine anywhere else she'd rather be. Couldn't imagine herself with any other man. Once, she'd thought Chad Russell was her ideal man. Now, she couldn't fathom that she ever had.

As her husband stood there so lost in thought, she felt a pang of sadness. No matter how wonderful their lovemaking, or how strong her desire to make him happy, she knew he kept a part of himself separate.

She'd known from the beginning, when she was trying so hard not to let her heart do something stupid and fall in love, that he had a core of loneliness he would not allow her to reach. It was his shield, his armor against the world.

She imagined breaking through it one day, imagined how it would be if he allowed himself to be completely free. She'd tried to talk to him about Chad and Elena a few times, but he shoved the conversation expertly aside each time. He didn't grow angry, the way he once had, but he also refused to allow it to take place.

Paige started up the steps, deciding that she'd spied on him long enough. He turned at the sound of her footsteps. His silver eyes, clouded with some emotion, cleared when he saw her.

"You have enjoyed your walk?" he asked.

She went to his side and leaned against the balustrade. "I did. It's quite refreshing to be able to enjoy a summer stroll without needing to shower and change afterward."

"It is very hot in Dallas now, isn't it?"

"Definitely. If I were there, I'd be inside with the AC cranked up on high and a glass of iced tea in my hand."

His smile was tender. "Don't let this weather fool you. We are located on the Gulf of Finland, so we do get hot and humid days during summer."

"I'll take a few days over several months," she said.

"Come, sit down and have some water." He took her hand and pulled her to the table. A crystal pitcher filled with sparkling water and sliced lemons sat on a cart beside it. He poured some into a goblet and handed it to her.

"Is everything okay, Alexei?" she asked after the silence stretched out between them.

He turned back to her, seeming to hesitate before speaking. She thought he would tell her that nothing was wrong, but he said, "Today is the fifteenth anniversary of my sister's death."

A little pang of feeling pierced her heart. He hadn't spoken of his sister since the first night when they'd eaten dinner together. Did this mean he was opening up to her? Or was she reading too much into it?

Her heart wanted to think he was beginning to feel for her the way she felt for him, but her head was more cautious.

"I'm sorry, Alexei. Do you want to talk about it?"

A gentle breeze stirred, blowing a napkin open where it lay on the table. Paige folded it over again and waited.

"Katerina had leukemia," he finally said. "She died because we couldn't afford the experimental treatment that might have saved her."

Her heart pinched. "I'm so sorry. That must have been hard for you and your mother."

"There was only me. My mother had advanced Alzheimer's by this time. She never knew what happened. She followed Katerina into the grave three years later. I am the only one left to remember any of them."

"There is still your aunt," she offered. She knew it was a risk, but she wanted him to realize that he really wasn't alone in this world. That he had the power to change things for them all. People made mistakes, but no one remained static over the years. His aunt might regret the way she'd felt about his mother now that she was older.

Alexei's face grew hard, closed off, and she knew she'd made a mistake.

Paige simply couldn't imagine cutting herself off from all her living family the way he had. She needed Emma, not just because they were sisters, but also because she saw her mother's beauty and grace in her sister's smile. Families were living reminders of those who had gone before.

But he did not see things the same as she did, and it saddened her.

"There is no possibility of reconciliation, Paige."

Stop right now, don't say it. But she couldn't leave it without stating the truth.

"Tim Russell is dead. Why let what he did stand between you and your family?"

"They are *not* my family." Alexei's voice cracked between them like a whip. Then he closed his eyes for a moment. "I'm sorry," he said when he opened them again. "It's not your fault."

Paige stood and went to him, wrapping her arms around his waist and burying her head against his chest. She couldn't stand to see him hurt, and she couldn't stand when she caused it by picking at his wounds. "I'm sorry, too. I didn't mean to hurt you."

Just when she thought he might push her away, his arms came around her and he squeezed her tight. "I know this."

"I just want to understand, Alexei." She wanted to understand so many things: why he was so adamant, why he couldn't let go of the past, why he kept himself closed in—and why, in spite of everything, she'd fallen in love with him.

His chest rumbled against her ear. "There is nothing to understand. It simply is."

Alexei couldn't sleep. Beside him, Paige's even breathing told him she'd had no such problem. Outside, the sky was white, but he had no idea what time it was. It could be midnight or it could be 3:00 a.m. They were in the middle of the *Beliye Nochi,* or White Nights, that St. Petersburg was famous for.

He pushed the covers back and got up, padding naked to the window to pull the thick curtains back and gaze at the sky.

Katerina had died on a night like this, when the sun never set and the world seemed bright and filled with eternal summer.

But there was no eternal summer, for Katerina or for

anyone. There was only a short season between dark, frozen, barren ones.

It scared him, that knowledge. It was why he'd refused to grow close to anyone else after the passing of his family. You couldn't hurt when you didn't care.

But Paige had taken that comfort away from him. Though he'd tried not to let it happen, she had grown important to him. He'd known when he'd returned to her side that night so many weeks ago that he was taking a chance. That once he touched her, he would not be able to let go.

She was all he needed. Paige and the baby. He did not need to reach out to Chad and Elena, though she wanted him to do so.

He only needed her. And he needed to explain to her why he could not cross that chasm, and why he'd had to destroy Russell Tech. The real reason, not the partial one he'd already told her. He wanted her to understand, and he wanted at last to tell another living person what he'd never said before. He *needed* to do so.

"Alexei?"

He turned to find her pushed up on one elbow, squinting toward the window. He let the curtain fall. "I'm sorry I woke you."

"No, it's fine. Please open the curtain again." She climbed from the bed and donned a robe while he did as she asked. She came to his side, yawning, and slipped an arm around his waist. "I'd heard about this, but it's hard to believe it never gets dark until you see it. It's the most amazing thing."

He was looking at the top of her dark head, her thick hair mussed from sleep and lovemaking, when she gazed up at him. "No, you are," he said softly.

She smiled, and his world lit from within. "You always know the right thing to say."

"Do I?"

"You must. You talked me into kissing you when I didn't know you, and you kept right on talking me into things until we ended up here."

"Perhaps I should have gone into politics."

Her smile grew more radiant, if that were possible. "It's probable we'd have world peace right this instant if you had."

Alexei grew serious. "I don't always know the right thing to say, *angel moy*."

"Perhaps not, but I'd wager you usually do."

If only that were true.

"When Katerina was dying, I went to Dallas," he said quickly, before he could change his mind.

The arm she'd wrapped around his waist tightened, as if she knew what he was about to say. She could not know, but he loved the way she sensed his turmoil. It comforted him, gave him the strength to continue.

"I went to see Tim Russell. I asked for his help, Paige. But he would not give it. He told me the Voronovs were dead to his wife, and therefore dead to him."

Her eyes glistened. "Oh, Alexei, I'm so sorry."

"She died in agony, because I could not save her. I tried, but I couldn't."

"It's not your fault," she said fiercely. Tears rolled down her cheeks now, and he cursed himself for making her cry. Why had he burdened her with this? He'd wanted to share it, but now that he had, he wished he could take it back. Anything to return the smile to her face.

"I've never told anyone what happened," he said thickly. "I didn't tell Katerina. It would have done her no good."

"You've carried this around by yourself for fifteen years? Oh, Alexei." She shook her head. "Why are you so stubborn?"

He blinked. Stubborn? Was he? "I had no reason to tell anyone, *lyubimaya moya*. This is not stubbornness."

She turned to him, put her hands on either side of his face. "But it is. You can't keep this kind of thing inside. It eats at you if you do. It's not healthy."

He put his hands over hers. "I'm not keeping it inside anymore, am I? You know—and now you know why I can never forgive the Russells. They took far more than land and money."

She lifted herself on tiptoe and pressed her mouth to his. He tasted the salt of her tears, and it sliced him open deep inside, both the knowledge he'd made her cry and the fact she was crying for him.

When she pulled back, her beautiful face was sad. He wanted to take her back to bed and make her forget everything he'd just told her. Why had he done it? And why did he feel as if a weight had been lifted now that he'd done so?

"You have to let this go," she said softly. "It's killing you."

He knew what she meant and he stiffened. "No, it has given me purpose. It has driven me to be what I am now." He spread his arms wide, encompassing their plush surroundings. "Without that purpose, I might not have any of this. And though I would trade it all for Katerina's life in a minute, I would not change what I have done to get here. Or what I will continue to do to keep this empire for you and our child."

"I don't want it at the expense of *you*," she cried. "Nothing is as important as—"

She stood there with wide eyes, her bottom lip trembling.

His heart thumped. "As important as what, Paige?"

"As you are to me," she finally said. "I love you, Alexei. Surely you know that by now."

His chest hurt. Absolutely hurt. Her words filled the empty

corners of his soul, made him ache with the sweetness and pain of it. She wasn't the first woman to say those words to him, and yet something about them coming from her was different.

Why?

A thread of panic began to unwind in his gut. How could he allow this to happen? Objectively he could say he needed her. That being with her made him happier than he'd been in a very long time. That hearing these words from her completed a missing part of him.

But emotionally he couldn't face the truth of it. Because need and love meant loss and pain and uncertainty. He'd vowed never to allow someone else's existence to determine his happiness. He knew from bitter experience that it would not turn out well.

"Aren't you going to say anything?" she asked, and he realized he'd remained silent too long. She searched his face, and though he wasn't certain what he saw there, he knew it wasn't what she wanted because the weight of sorrow bracketed her mouth once more.

"What do you wish me to say?" As if he didn't know. But he couldn't do it, couldn't tell her something that he feared would swallow him whole if he said it. The words wouldn't come—and he wasn't sure he wanted them to.

She clutched her robe tighter around her body. "Nothing, Alexei. Nothing at all."

"You need to sleep," he said gruffly. Because he'd hurt her again, and because he hated doing so. "The baby needs you to be healthy."

She flinched as if he'd hit her. "The baby. Yes, of course." Her hand had settled over her abdomen.

He didn't know what to say. It was within his power to reverse this. To tell her what she wanted to hear and to make her smile again. But it was impossible to do so.

She walked over to the bed and shed her robe. He followed, turning her in his arms and hauling her close before she could lie down again. Her body was stiff with rejection and he thought, for a moment, it would kill him.

"I'm tired," she said softly, her voice heavy with emotion.

He held her for a moment longer, his heart thumping in his breast like a trapped eagle beating its wings against a cage. He knew what he needed to say, what would make everything right again—

He let her go. And then, because he deserved the torture, he spent the rest of the night beside her, not touching her, knowing she was lying as far from him as she could possibly get without falling out of the bed.

When Paige woke the next morning, Alexei was gone. It wasn't the first morning she'd awakened and he wasn't there, but this morning was different. She knew it in her bones. After last night, after her stupidity in confessing her love to him, she'd known he would be gone.

But part of her had hoped he wouldn't be. She'd let her emotions get the best of her, when he'd told her with such pain in his voice about his sister and about Chad's father's cruelty to them. She'd hated Tim Russell for him in that moment.

She'd understood, in a way she'd have never thought possible, what had driven him to ruin Russell Tech. And it horrified her, feeling those emotions. If it horrified her after feeling it for only a few minutes, what must it be like to live with that feeling for fifteen years?

She'd wanted him to understand how damaging those emotions were, but she hadn't meant to tell him she loved him. Not yet. It was too new, too fragile, and she'd feared he didn't feel the same way. They'd had a wonderful few weeks together, but that wasn't enough to build a lifetime of love on.

Paige groaned as she stood in front of the mirror, brushing her hair. The look on his face when she'd told him she loved him—oh, God. You'd have thought she'd told him the world was ending tomorrow at noon he'd looked so horrified.

He didn't love her, didn't need her. He'd married her for the baby, and he enjoyed the sex. Sometimes, he even enjoyed the companionship.

But why had he told her about the dark things in his life if he didn't care?

Paige dropped the brush and whirled from the mirror before she drove herself insane. She didn't understand anything about the man she'd married. Just when she thought she did, he stunned her with the evidence that she'd had it all wrong. When he'd told her she needed to sleep for the sake of the baby, she'd felt like he'd slapped her. She'd been stunned, hurt and numb.

When he'd tried to hold her, she'd wanted to be in his arms—and yet she'd known she couldn't survive it. She'd hated the way they'd ended last night. She'd hated lying on the edge of the bed, aching for him to touch her and knowing he would not once she'd rejected him. Knowing that she would fall apart if he did so. Because he didn't love her, and she loved him desperately.

And now he was gone and she was cursing herself for spilling her love so carelessly. If she'd said nothing, they would have continued the way they had been.

But, she asked herself angrily, was that enough? Didn't she deserve more?

She emerged into their suite to find a maid setting the table outside on the terrace with a full breakfast. She wasn't sure she was all that hungry, but for the baby's sake she knew she needed to eat.

"Dobroye Utro," she said to the woman, who curtsied and

returned the greeting before picking up her tray and hurrying away.

A cream envelope lay beside her plate. She picked it up and sliced it open with a butter knife. She already knew what it was. The only mystery was how he would phrase the need for his absence.

Have to go into Moscow this morning. Will return tonight.
Alexei

She stared toward the Gulf of Finland in the distance, her insides churning with a riot of love, pain and fury. The morning sunshine sparkled on the water like millions of winking diamonds. Would one night turn into two? Would it become a week, and then a month, and then two months before she saw him again? Had she chased him away with her naive declaration?

Because how could a man like Alexei love her? He was handsome, successful and utterly ruthless with his enemies. He'd married her out of a sense of duty, nothing more. No matter what he said to the contrary, he belonged with a woman like the Countess Kozlova—someone elegant and accustomed to his world.

No. That was ridiculous. She was being emotional and stupid and, worse, indulging in self-pity. Paige crumpled the envelope in her fist before she set it on the table and smoothed it flat again.

There was a fluttering in her stomach, so soft and light that she ignored it at first. And then it happened again. It felt like a tiny bird, like a butterfly. She realized with a sense of wonder that it was her baby moving.

Her resolve hardened. No more self-pity. No more waiting on the sidelines for Alexei to figure out how he felt.

Because she was worthy of love, and she was worthy of this man. And she was not about to let him evade her this time.

CHAPTER THIRTEEN

IT HADN'T BEEN easy to get to Moscow, but Paige had refused to take no for an answer. First, she'd ordered a car to go shopping—without Mariya there, she'd managed to get away without a security detail. Then she'd made the driver take her to the airport where she'd found an English-speaking ticket agent—in truth, they all seemed to speak English—and bought a ticket to Moscow on the earliest flight she could get.

She had a bit of difficulty finding a driver to take her to Voronov Exploration's headquarters, but she finally managed that as well. Now, she sat in the limo speeding into Moscow and wondered if she'd gone too far.

Alexei would be furious. Her heart had been racing since she'd begun the journey, and now her stomach was upset as well. A sharp pang sliced beneath her kidney, nearly doubling her over. She should have eaten something more than a boiled egg and a glass of milk.

When the driver pulled in front of the soaring glass and steel building in the Presnensky district, Paige counted out the rubles from her purse and stepped onto the sidewalk. The noise of the city was somewhat jarring after she'd spent so many quiet weeks in the country. Cars shot by, the older ones belching fumes, and men and women hurried up and down the sidewalks, talking on cell phones, gesturing wildly as they strode along. She remembered that life, though it seemed like a distant memory now. Once, she'd been the one in a suit and tennis shoes, rushing down the sidewalk with a tray of coffee she'd picked up at the nearest Starbucks.

She didn't miss the economic uncertainty of that life, but she did miss Mavis and the other friends she'd made at work. Even Mr. Ramirez, who she'd barely known. He'd been so kind to her when she was new and ill, before she found out she was pregnant. He'd paid her the hours, as he'd said he would, but when she cashed the check, she sent that portion back since she hadn't earned it.

She missed that life in some ways, the one where she mattered to people and where they valued her. She wanted Alexei to value her. But if he did not, if he would not, she was better off in Dallas, sitting in her cubicle and struggling to make ends meet. At least her life would be her own. Though it pained her to think it, she knew she had the strength. She loved Alexei, but if he did not—or would not—love her, then she would insist on making her own choices instead of meekly waiting in St. Petersburg for him to return.

Paige went into the sleek lobby and marched up to the front desk. A woman with a headset looked up, smiled briefly and then continued talking on the phone. When she finally finished, she asked what she could do to help.

"I'm here to see Prince Voronov," Paige said.

Even the woman's frown was friendly. "I am afraid that is not possible, madam. His schedule is booked solid today. If you would care to make an appointment?"

"No, I would not. I am his wife, and I want to see him now, please." She tried so hard to be cool and collected, but her stomach was burning and she realized now how ridiculous it seemed for a woman to march into the lobby and claim to be Alexei's wife. If she truly were his wife, wouldn't she know where to go and how to find him? Wouldn't she at least have his cell phone number?

The woman smiled the bland, noncommittal smile of an efficient receptionist. "Please wait over there," she said, gesturing to a row of low bench seats along one glass wall.

Paige started to argue, but what good would it do? Instead she marched over and sank onto the white leather bench as gracefully as she could manage. She was beginning to wish she'd stayed in St. Petersburg. At least she could lie in bed and wait for this queasiness to go away.

She didn't know how long she waited, but she knew before he arrived that he'd come for her. There was an electric disturbance in the air, the crackle and snap of fury that preceded him like a wave.

And then he was in the lobby, striding toward her, his face dark and hard.

"Are you out of your mind?" he snapped, the words cracking through the air like a whip.

"Maybe I am," she said. She wanted to get up and jab her finger into his chest, to demand to know why he'd left, but she didn't have the energy.

She'd come here to be strong, to demand he not withdraw from the life they'd been building. She'd come here to assert herself and fight for her husband.

But now she was tired and aching and she just wanted to lie down and sleep. Perhaps she'd picked up a summer cold, or eaten something bad.

He reached for her. "Come, I'm sending you to my apartment. When I'm finished here, I'll join you."

"Fine," she said, though she wasn't sure she believed him. He would board a plane to St. Petersburg and leave her here, she was certain. Anything to get away from her.

Even with his hand on her elbow, it was a struggle to stand. It took her a moment to realize that she was wet, that she must have sat in someone's spilled drink. Why hadn't she noticed when she first sat down?

"Alexei," she started to say.

But the color drained from his face until he was as white as the bench seat. "My God, Paige," he croaked.

She followed his gaze downward as warmth spread along her legs. It took her a moment to understand the meaning of the small drops of red on the floor between her feet. When she did, a cracked scream wrenched from her suddenly dry throat.

It was all his fault. He'd been a fool, an ass, an arrogant unfeeling brute. Alexei shoved trembling fingers through his hair. Why had he left her like that? Why hadn't he realized it was the wrong thing to do? Why hadn't he brought her with him? He'd intended to go back tonight, but if he were honest with himself, he knew he'd have found a reason not to.

Why?

Because he was a coward. Because he didn't want to face his feelings and fears. He was very good at running from emotions he didn't want to feel. He'd been doing it for years, subsisting on hate and ambition, and it had finally taken its toll.

Not only on him, but also on Paige and their child.

In that moment when he'd seen the blood on the seat and floor, he'd believed his world had come crashing down around him. He'd thought he was losing her, and he'd offered up everything he had—every ruble, every ounce of success, *everything*—if only God would listen to his plea and spare her life.

Someone had listened, because she was fine. She and the baby both. Relief had made him so weak he couldn't stand when the doctor gave him the news. The bleeding was stabilized, and there had been no contractions, which was a good sign. The doctor said she could go home, but she was on strict bed rest for the next month.

A nurse came and told him he could go into Paige's room now. Alexei pushed open the door to find Paige sitting on the bed, dressed in the clothes he'd had sent over for her, her hands clenched in her lap.

His throat closed up. "You look pale, *lyubimaya moya.*"

"I'm sorry, Alexei," she said, her eyes red and swollen from crying. "I put our baby in danger and I can never forgive myself—"

Her voice broke and he went and wrapped his arms around her, tucked her head against his chest. His heart raced as he stroked the glorious, fragrant silk of her hair. "Do not cry, Paige. It's bad for the baby."

She made a strangled sound against him. He felt the reverberations through his body and knew that, once more, he'd said the wrong thing.

"It's bad for you, too," he amended. "Please don't do anything that's bad for you."

She clutched his shirt as she took deep, steadying breaths. "No, of course. You're right. I have to be careful, for both of us."

"For all of us."

They stayed like that for a long time, with him stroking her hair, and her holding tight to him.

"I didn't want you to stay away," she said softly. "That's why I followed you to Moscow. I don't want to do this alone, Alexei. I want what we've had for the past few weeks."

He couldn't speak, could only hold her close and comfort himself with the rhythmic rise and fall of her chest. She was alive, breathing.

She pushed away from him. He let her go, uncertain of what she wanted from him and unwilling to upset her again.

She looked so beautiful sitting there, so pale and fragile, that he wanted to pull her into his arms again and never let go.

"No, that's not true," she said, shaking her head, and his heart dropped. She'd decided that she didn't love him, that she didn't need or want him after all. It was his punishment for what he'd put her through, for his stubbornness and inability to see the truth.

"Tell me what you want and it is yours," he said. Even if she wanted to leave him, he would do his utmost to allow her to go. Whatever it took to make her happy.

Her expression grew suddenly fierce. "I want *more,* Alexei. I want you to feel what I feel. I don't want to live with a man who doesn't love me. I've spent my adult life pleasing others, and I'm ready for someone to please *me*. It's my turn to have it all. And if you can't give that to me, then I want to know it. Because, though I love you, I won't stay in your palace and your bed and hope that one day you'll love me, too."

She was so fierce, his wife. So amazing and fierce and wonderful. And he would do anything to make her happy. *Anything*.

The feeling sweeping through him was so strong that his vision narrowed, as if he would collapse if he didn't give it voice. "I love you," he said. But the words sounded choked, rusted through. "I love you," he said again, stronger this time.

She looked hopeful. And then, just as quickly, hope faded. "You're just saying it because you know I want to hear it."

He couldn't blame her for thinking such a thing. She knew him to be ruthless and determined, willing to use her for information, willing to do whatever it took to win. Why wouldn't he say the words he knew she wanted to hear if it benefited him to do so?

He had to make her believe, had to prove to her how hard this was for him and how utterly certain he was that it was right. Alexei dropped to his knees in front of her. Her eyes widened as he clasped her hands in his. Then he bent until his forehead touched her knees.

"I'm no good at this," he said, his heart feeling like a dead weight in his chest. "I don't know how to tell you that you are the most important thing to me, that I was dead inside until you crashed into my life. I don't know how to say the right words, Paige. *Ti nuzhna mne, ya tebya lyublyu.* That is all I have, all I know."

"What did you say to me?" she asked, her voice soft and thready.

He looked up, his gaze clashing with hers. "I said that I need you, that I love you."

"I want to believe you, but so much has happened, Alexei." Her smoky eyes were sad, haunted.

"For you," he vowed, "I will go to see Chad and Elena."

She withdrew her hand from his grip, smoothed it along his jaw. "Oh, Alexei." Her eyes filled with new tears. It gave him hope like he'd never had before. "I want you to see them because *you* want to, because *you* believe it will enrich your life to do so, but not because it's something you think I expect of you."

He understood what she was saying, and yet he knew that it was right. That he wanted to do this for himself as much as for her and their child.

"I've had time to consider many things these past few hours," he told her. "When I thought I might lose you, I realized how closed off I have become, how alone. I thought you and the baby would be enough for me—and you are—but I also realized that you are right. I have hated the Russells for fifteen years, and I believed they hated me. Perhaps they still do. But I'm tired of hating. I have no more use for it."

He drew in a breath, more certain of this than he'd ever been. "I will see them, Paige, because you have convinced me it is the right thing to do. And I will know, once I've done so, that no matter what happens, I made the effort."

"You really mean it," she said wonderingly.

"*Da,* I do."

"But why do you love me *now,*" she said, as if she still couldn't fathom that he could truly be in love with her. "If you are simply trying to keep me happy until the baby comes, I'd rather you didn't. I don't want to be lied to."

Alexei got to his feet. This part was easy, comparatively speaking. "I understand why you are skeptical," he said. He spread a hand along her jaw, cupped her lovely face as he skimmed his thumb over her cheek, her soft brow. "But, Paige, I have been drawn to you from the first moment I met you. You are unlike anyone I've ever known. You are so fierce and strong, yet you don't seem to always know it. You are uncertain of yourself sometimes, uncertain of your beauty and appeal, and you have the kindest heart of anyone I know. You cry over art, you laugh like an angel, and you'd fight to the death to protect those you love."

The tears were flowing down her cheeks now, and he wiped them away with his thumbs. "Shh, please don't cry, Paige. It breaks my heart when you cry."

"I can't help it," she said, shaking her head.

"I love you, Paige, and it terrifies me to say this. Because everyone I've ever loved has left me, and I've had to carry on without them, missing them, knowing I failed to do all I could for them. I don't wish to fail you, Paige, or to live without you. I need you too much."

She wrapped her arms around him and hugged him tight. "I love you, Alexei. So much. And I don't believe we need to be scared of love. We have to take what it gives us and be happy. If we do that, we can't fail. Just as you didn't fail Katerina. She knew you loved her, and though I know you wish she had lived, it's not your fault she didn't. It really, truly isn't. I want you to believe that."

He smiled at her, his heart opening so wide it hurt. The love was overwhelming once he let it in, and the fear faded by degrees until all it could do was sit in a corner and look out at the unfolding scene. Fear would always be there, he knew, but it wasn't the biggest thing in the room anymore.

"I will try to believe it, *lyubimaya moya*. For you."

"No," she said fiercely. "For you."

"Yes," he said. "For me." Because she was right. Because she knew him so well, and loved him so much, and because he wasn't afraid to face his fear any longer.

Dallas in winter was far more pleasant than St. Petersburg. The temperatures were mild compared to the subzero temperatures of Russia. And yet Paige missed Russia, too. She missed the huge, elegant Voronov Palace and she missed the winter *troika* rides. But they would return in the early spring, when snow was still on the ground and the weather was not so severe.

"The baby is asleep," Emma announced as she returned from the room where she'd taken little Katerina for a nap.

"She's a good baby," Paige said. "She hardly fusses at all."

Emma sat down on the couch beside her. "She is so perfect, Paige. You are very lucky."

Paige smiled. She *was* lucky. Lucky to have her wonderful baby and lucky to have a husband she adored. A husband who bought her a house in Dallas and moved them there for the winter because he knew she was homesick.

The house he'd bought for them wasn't as vast as Paige had feared it might be, because she'd begged him to find something approximating normal. And he had. They'd found a gorgeous classical architecture house in the historic district that she absolutely loved. The trees would be huge and shady in summer and the front porch ran the full length of the home. There was plenty of room for furniture and sitting out in the evenings when the weather warmed a little bit more.

She'd had to explain the Southern tradition of sitting out on the front porch and greeting neighbors to Alexei. He hadn't exactly understood the necessity, but he'd kissed her and told her that whatever she wanted, he would get for her.

Emma glanced toward the patio. "Are they still out there?"

Paige laughed. "Yes. I believe Chad is explaining how to smoke a whole hog in a pit." She'd heard them talking when she'd gone into the kitchen to refresh her drink.

Emma rolled her eyes. "They're supposed to be grilling steaks. How did that happen?"

"I'm not sure, but Chad seems determined to teach Alexei what it means to be a true Texan. Barbecue is high on the list, it would seem."

In the last eight months, Alexei had made good on his promise to contact Chad and Elena. He and Chad were slowly building a relationship, though it couldn't be called easy or smooth by any means. Unfortunately Elena was a bitter woman who would probably carry her disapproval of Alexei and his mother to her grave. Alexei did not seem to care, which was a relief to Paige even if it hurt her that the woman couldn't acknowledge her nephew.

Chad, however, seemed eager to get to know his cousin once he'd gotten over the shock of Alexei actually offering an olive branch. Alexei hadn't told Chad what his father had done, nor would he. Paige understood, and though she already loved Alexei to distraction, that single act of nobility and selflessness made her so proud to be his wife.

He was a good, good man.

"Chad told me that Alexei offered him a position overseeing

the American branch of his operations," Emma said, twisting a lock of her long hair as she did so.

"I believe the man who'd been in the position retired recently," Paige replied. "And Chad has the experience."

"Thank you for talking him into it," Emma said. "It means a lot to us both."

"I didn't talk him into anything, Emma. And Alexei would do nothing to harm his business. If he offered the job to Chad, then he believes Chad is right for the position."

Emma stretched, grinning. "Whatever. I don't care so long as it means we can finally be married."

Just then, the men came back into the house, speaking rapidly in a combination of Russian and English. Chad carried a platter of steaks in one hand and a beer in the other. Alexei was loaded down with grilling implements that he dumped into the sink.

They spent the evening eating, talking and laughing together like a group of old friends. Paige glanced over at Alexei, loving the way he was so animated and open, the way he seemed to truly take pleasure in Chad's company. It was a far cry from the way the two men had once looked at each other across a table.

Later, while Chad and Emma carried the dishes into the kitchen, Alexei turned to her. His expression changed, became possessive and sensual as his hungry gaze slipped over her. Her insides liquefied, softened. She wanted him as much, if not more, than she ever had. When he looked at her like that, like she was everything in the world to him, she melted.

He leaned toward her, kissed her softly—much more softly than she would have liked when she was absolutely on fire for him.

"Thank you," he said.

She wrapped her arms around his neck, unwilling to let him go just yet. "For what?"

"For making my life so much more than I ever thought possible."

Her heart swelled with love and longing. "I'm not done yet," she murmured. "I have a lot more to show you. Starting as soon as our guests have left."

His grin was feral, hot and sexy. "I look forward to it," he growled. "Because I have a few things to show you as well."

Paige laughed. "Bring it on, big boy."

Hours later, when Paige lay in bed exhausted and happy, she knew she would never, ever tire of life with this man.

"I love you," she whispered against his hot, damp skin.

He kissed her shoulder, her throat, her lips. *"Ya tebya lyublyu,"* he replied. "More than you will ever know."

And then he showed her again, without words, how much he loved her.

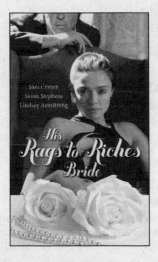

FLORA'S DEFIANCE
by Lynne Graham

Angelo Van Zaal is convinced he should have guardianship of Flora Bennett's niece, despite Flora wanting to adopt too. There has to be a way to make Flora concede to his wishes... *and* indulge his infuriating attraction to her...

THE WEDDING CHARADE
by Melanie Milburne

Nic Sabbatini doesn't respond well to ultimatums. But when stunning Jade Sommerville announces their upcoming nuptials to the media, he may have finally met his match!

HER UNKNOWN HEIR
by Chantelle Shaw

Two years after their fling ended, Ramon Velaquez can't forget Lauren Maitland, the woman he banished. But when he finds her again, she's strong, independent, and harbouring a secret...

THE INHERITED BRIDE
By Maisey Yates

Princess Isabella didn't want to marry the Sheikh to whom she was betrothed. But after her sensual journey to the desert she was never going to be the same again...

On sale from 21st January 2011
Don't miss out!

THE RELUCTANT DUKE
by Carole Mortimer

Forced to return to his family's seat, Lucan St Claire takes beautiful PA Lexie Hamilton with him. Lucan, however, has no idea that his new assistant isn't quite what she seems...

THE DEVIL WEARS KOLOVSKY
by Carol Marinelli

Swearing revenge on the Kolovskys, who abandoned him, Zakahr Belenki determines to destroy their fashion empire! Then he meets his secretary, Lavinia. Her honesty and passion for her job make Zakahr's conscience waver—and inflame his desire...

PRINCESS FROM THE PAST
by Caitlin Crews

Marriage to Prince Leo Di Marco was no fairytale, so Bethany Vassal ran away, hoping the man she loved would come and find her. Now the time has come for Leo to produce a royal heir— and Bethany must return to the castle whence she fled!

INTERVIEW WITH A PLAYBOY
by Kathryn Ross

Marco Lombardi *hates* journalists. Whisking reporter Isobel Keyes away in luxury seems like damage limitation—until she sparks his interest. Now Marco *wants* to kiss and tell...

On sale from 4th February 2011
Don't miss out!

Available at WHSmith, Tesco, ASDA, Eason and all good bookshops

www.millsandboon.co.uk

are proud to present our...

Book of the Month

Prince Voronov's Virgin
by Lynn Raye Harris

from Mills & Boon® Modern™

Paige Barnes is rescued from the dark streets of
Moscow by Prince Alexei Voronov—her boss's
deadliest rival.   Now he has Paige unexpectedly in
his sights, Alexei will play emotional Russian
roulette to keep her close…

Available 17th December

Something to say about our Book of the Month?
Tell us what you think!

millsandboon.co.uk/community
facebook.com/romancehq
twitter.com/millsandboonuk

2 FREE BOOKS
AND A SURPRISE GIFT

We would like to take this opportunity to thank you for reading this Mills & Boon® book by offering you the chance to take TWO more specially selected books from the Modern™ series absolutely FREE! We're also making this offer to introduce you to the benefits of the Mills & Boon® Book Club™—

- **FREE home delivery**
- **FREE gifts and competitions**
- **FREE monthly Newsletter**
- **Exclusive Mills & Boon Book Club offers**
- **Books available before they're in the shops**

Accepting these FREE books and gift places you under no obligation to buy, you may cancel at any time, even after receiving your free books. Simply complete your details below and return the entire page to the address below. You don't even need a stamp!

YES Please send me 2 free Modern books and a surprise gift. I understand that unless you hear from me, I will receive 4 superb new books every month for just £3.30 each, postage and packing free. I am under no obligation to purchase any books and may cancel my subscription at any time. The free books and gift will be mine to keep in any case.

Ms/Mrs/Miss/Mr _____ Initials _____

Surname _____

Address _____

_____

_____ Postcode _____

E-mail _____

Send this whole page to: Mills & Boon Book Club, Free Book Offer, FREEPOST NAT 10298, Richmond, TW9 1BR